MW00464825

BISON FRONTIERS OF IMAGINATION

THE WONDER

J. D. BERESFORD

Introduction to the Bison Books Edition by
Jack L. Chalker

UNIVERSITY OF NEBRASKA PRESS
LINCOLN AND LONDON

♾

First Bison Books printing: 1999
Most recent printing indicated by the last digit below:
10   9   8   7   6   5   4   3   2   1

Library of Congress Cataloging-in-Publication Data
Beresford, J. D. (John Davys), 1873–1947.
[Hampdenshire wonder]
The wonder / by J. D. Beresford; introduction to the Bison
Books edition by Jack L. Chalker.
p.   cm.—(Bison frontiers of imagination)
ISBN 0-8032-6162-4 (pbk.: alk. paper)
I. Title.   II. Series.
PR6003.E73H36   1999
823′.912—dc21
99-35542   CIP

To

MY FRIEND AND CRITIC

ARTHUR SCOTT CRAVEN

OUTSIDERS: AN INTRODUCTION

JACK L. CHALKER

There are the conformists and the approved and the outsiders. I suspect that this has always been a sociological fact, but it resonates because we all feel it. The non-athlete in a school that prizes athletics; the one with too big a nose, or odd *evil* eyes, or who's too fat, too thin, too withdrawn, too—*weird*. The cause may be physiological, sociological, or psychological, but we've all felt it, been a part of it, sometimes on not one but *both* sides of it.

When we are the outsider, though, we tend in some ways to cope, making assets of that which "they" make fun of, retreating into fantasy where the social disjointedness turns out to be symptoms of something grand, glorious, new, and different. The Ugly Duckling turns into a beautiful swan; his tormentors grow up to be mere *ducks*.

It's rarely if ever true, but it helps. You cope with it, and you learn how to be more accepting of who and what you are.

But what if it were true? What if the outsider was indeed not a retro step, not a defect, but rather something grander, something greater, something both awesome and, yes, scary. It's a common theme in science fiction, that form that is most useful when you have something to say and need a bit of distance to properly say it. The theme exists because we continue to act the way we do against the outsiders, and we don't seem to ever learn, just now and then change targets.

Perhaps the most famous example of this in literature is Olaf Stapleton's *Odd John*, often considered the base from which all others in this sub-genre spring. But Stapleton, one of the greatest writers in the science fiction genre, was in this case standing on an older foundation, John Davys Beresford's *The Wonder* (originally titled *The Hampdenshire Wonder*).

Beresford's novel is at once a pioneering work of science fiction, a look at the outsider syndrome, and an unintended psychological study. Beresford was crippled by polio early in life and grew up with this condition. He had to watch the other children at athletic play and probably endure some unintended cruelty from remarks of the unaffected children he wanted to join. This more than anything shaped a lot of his work, from the solid science fiction of *Wonder* to the fantasy novel of faith healing, *The Camerwell Miracle*. A clergyman's son, he believed in miracles, but a modern man, he also saw the potential of science.

The most remarkable thing about *The Wonder* is how solidly science fiction it is. This is a story of mutation and, as such, of implicit acceptance of evolution and its unspoken future potential. There are no contractions here in Beresford's mind or writing between the scientific and the spiritual; the twisting and distortion is done by the bigotry and hardness of views of individual human beings, not by the basics of his universe. For 1911, this is pretty solid science fiction.

What is also interesting about this whole genre of the superman born before his time is how the lineal descendants echo many of the attitudes of their times. *Wonder* holds up remarkably well, but it is very much in period as an expression of an age that sees potential in everything and an ever brighter future. The *Titanic* is still a year away. *Odd John* is later, its author knows better, and it is a darker work. Other lineal descendants, from the symbol of hope in the Depression, Superman himself, to Norvill Page's post-Hiroshima *But Without Horns* and Frank M. Robinson's *The Power* reflecting fifties paranoia, say as much about the culture and atmosphere in which they were written as they do about what future products of human evolution (if any) might really be like. In the end, these tales of the outsider with power are not about the future of humankind but rather about the times and cultures in which they were written.

And, just as important, perhaps even *more* important, is how the reader reacts to the super outsider.

Sit back, relax, and read this book not as a historical curiosity or a psychology lesson but rather as a very good story that's quite well told. You'll be entertained, even if transported to a different place and time. It's only when you've finished, and can think about what might have disturbed you in the tale, that you'll discover, as all the best stories help you to do, something unexpected in yourself.

CONTENTS

PART I

MY EARLY ASSOCIATIONS WITH GINGER STOTT

PART II

THE CHILDHOOD OF THE WONDER

PART II (*continued*)

THE WONDER AMONG BOOKS

PART III

MY ASSOCIATION WITH THE WONDER

PART I

MY EARLY ASSOCIATIONS
WITH GINGER STOTT

CHAPTER I

I

I COULD not say at which station the woman and her baby entered the train.

Since we had left London I had been engrossed in Henri Bergson's " Time and Free Will," as it is called in the English translation. I had been conscious of various stoppages and changes of passengers, but my attention had been held by Bergson's argument. I agreed with his conclusion in advance, but I wished to master his reasoning.

I looked up when the woman entered my compartment, though I did not notice the name of the station. I caught sight of the baby she was carrying, and turned back to my book. I thought the child was a freak, an abnormality; and such things disgust me.

I returned to the study of my Bergson and read : " It is at the great and solemn crisis, de-

3

cisive of our reputation with others, that we choose in defiance of what is conventionally called a motive, and this absence of any tangible reason is the more striking the deeper our freedom goes.''

I kept my eyes on the book—the train had started again—but the next passage conveyed no meaning to my mind, and as I attempted to re-read it an impression was interposed between me and the work I was studying.

I saw projected on the page before me an image which I mistook at first for the likeness of Richard Owen. It was the conformation of the head that gave rise to the mistake, a head domed and massive, white and smooth—it was a head that had always interested me. But as I looked, my mind already searching for the reason of this hallucination, I saw that the lower part of the face was that of an infant. My eyes wandered from the book, and my gaze fluttered along the four persons seated opposite to me, till they rested on the reality of my vision. Even as these acts were being performed, I found myself foolishly saying, '' I don't call this freedom.''

For several seconds the eyes of the infant held mine. Its gaze was steady and clear as that of a normal child, but what differentiated it was the impression one received of calm intelligence. The head was completely bald, and there was no trace of eyebrows, but the eyes themselves were protected by thick, short lashes.

The child turned its head, and I felt my muscles relax. Until then I had not been conscious that they had been stiffened. My gaze was released, pushed aside as it were, and I found myself watching the object of the child's next scrutiny.

This object was a man of forty or so, inclined to corpulence, and untidy. He bore the evidences of failure in the process of becoming. He wore a beard that was scanty and ragged, there were bare patches of skin on the jaw; one inferred that he wore that beard only to save the trouble of shaving. He was sitting next to me, the middle passenger of the three on my side of the carriage, and he was absorbed in the pages of a half-penny paper—I think he was reading the Police News—which was interposed between him and the child in the corner diagonally opposite to that which I occupied.

The man was hunched up, slouching, his legs crossed, his elbows seeking support against his body; he held with both hands his paper, unfolded, close to his eyes. He had the appearance of being very myopic, but he did not wear glasses.

As I watched him, he began to fidget. He uncrossed his legs and hunched his body deeper into the back of his seat. Presently his eyes began to creep up the paper in front of him. When they reached the top, he hesitated a moment, making a survey under cover, then he dropped his hands and stared stupidly at the infant in the corner, his mouth slightly open, his feet pulled in under the seat of the carriage.

As the child let him go, his head drooped, and then he turned and looked at me with a silly, vacuous smile. I looked away hurriedly; this was not a man with whom I cared to share experience.

The process was repeated. The next victim was a big, rubicund, healthy-looking man, clean shaved, with light-blue eyes that were slightly magnified by the glasses of his gold-mounted spectacles. He, too, had been reading a newspaper —the *Evening Standard*—until the child's gaze claimed his attention, and he, too, was held motionless by that strange, appraising stare. But when he was released, his surprise found vent in words. "This," I thought, "is the man accustomed to act."

"A very remarkable child, ma'am," he said, addressing the thin, ascetic-looking mother.

II

The mother's appearance did not convey the impression of poverty. She was, indeed, warmly, decently, and becomingly clad. She wore a long black coat, braided and frogged; it had the air of belonging to an older fashion, but the material of it was new. And her bonnet, trimmed with jet ornaments growing on stalks that waved tremulously—that, also, was a modern replica of an older mode. On her hands were black thread gloves, somewhat ill-fitting.

Her face was not that of a country woman. The thin, high-bridged nose, the fallen cheeks, the shadows under eyes gloomy and retrospective— these were marks of the town; above all, perhaps, that sallow greyness of the skin which speaks of confinement. . . .

The child looked healthy enough. Its great bald head shone resplendently like a globe of alabaster.

" A very remarkable child, ma'am," said the rubicund man who sat facing the woman.

The woman twitched her untidy-looking black eyebrows, her head trembled slightly and set the jet fruit of her bonnet dancing and nodding.

" Yes, sir," she replied.

" Very remarkable," said the man, adjusting his spectacles and leaning forward. His action had an air of deliberate courage; he was justifying his fortitude after that temporary aberration.

I watched him a little nervously. I remembered

my feelings when, as a child, I had seen some magnificent enter the lion's den in a travelling circus. The failure on my right was, also, absorbed in the spectacle ; he stared, open-mouthed, his eyes blinking and shifting.

The other three occupants of the compartment, sitting on the same side as the woman, back to the engine, dropped papers and magazines and turned their heads, all interest. None of these three had, so far as I had observed, fallen under the spell of inspection by the infant, but I noticed that the man—an artisan apparently—who sat next to the woman had edged away from her, and that the three passengers opposite to me were huddled towards my end of the compartment.

The child had abstracted its gaze, which was now directed down the aisle of the carriage, indefinitely focussed on some point outside the window. It seemed remote, entirely unconcerned with any human being.

I speak of it asexually. I was still uncertain as to its sex. It is true that all babies look alike to me; but I should have known that this child was male, the conformation of the skull alone should have told me that. It was its dress that gave me cause to hesitate. It was dressed absurdly, not in " long-clothes," but in a long frock that hid its feet and was bunched about its body.

III

" Er—does it—er—can it—talk ? " hesitated the rubicund man, and I grew hot at his boldness. There seemed to be something disrespectful in speaking before the child in this impersonal way.

" No, sir, he's never made a sound," replied the woman, twitching and vibrating. Her heavy, dark eyebrows jerked spasmodically, nervously.

" Never cried ? " persisted the interrogator.

" Never once, sir."

" Dumb, eh ? " He said it as an aside, half under his breath.

" 'E's never spoke, sir."

" Hm ! " The man cleared his throat and braced himself with a deliberate and obvious effort. " Is it—he—not water on the brain—what ? "

I felt that a rigour of breathless suspense held every occupant of the compartment. I wanted, and I know that every other person there wanted, to say, " Look out ! Don't go too far." The child, however, seemed unconscious of the insult : he still stared out through the window, lost in profound contemplation.

" No, sir, oh no ! " replied the woman. " 'E's got more sense than a ordinary child." She held the infant as if it were some priceless piece of earthenware, not nursing it as a woman nurses a baby, but balancing it with supreme attention in her lap.

" How old is he ? "

We had been awaiting this question.

" A year and nine munse, sir."

" Ought to have spoken before that, oughtn't he ? "

" Never even cried, sir," said the woman. She regarded the child with a look into which I read something of apprehension. If it were apprehension it was a feeling that we all shared. But the rubicund man was magnificent, though, like the lion tamer of my youthful experience, he was doubtless conscious of the aspect his temerity wore in the eyes of beholders. He must have been showing off.

" Have you taken opinion ? " he asked ; and then, seeing the woman's lack of comprehension, he translated the question—badly, for he conveyed a different meaning—thus,

" I mean, have you had a doctor for him?"

The train was slackening speed.

" Oh ! yes, sir."

" And what do *they* say ? "

The child turned its head and looked the rubicund man full in the eyes. Never in the face of any man or woman have I seen such an expression of sublime pity and contempt. . . .

I remembered a small urchin I had once seen at

the Zoological Gardens. Urged on by a band of other urchins, he was throwing pebbles at a great lion that lolled, finely indifferent, on the floor of its playground. Closer crept the urchin; he grew splendidly bold; he threw larger and larger pebbles, until the lion rose suddenly with a roar, and dashed fiercely down to the bars of its cage.

I thought of that urchin's scared, shrieking face now, as the rubicund man leant quickly back into his corner.

Yet that was not all, for the infant, satisfied, perhaps, with its victim's ignominy, turned and looked at me with a cynical smile. I was, as it were, taken into its confidence. I felt flattered, undeservedly yet enormously flattered. I blushed, I may have simpered.

The train drew up in Great Hittenden station.

The woman gathered her priceless possession carefully into her arms, and the rubicund man adroitly opened the door for her.

" Good day, sir," she said, as she got out.

" Good day," echoed the rubicund man with relief, and we all drew a deep breath of relief with him in concert, as though we had just witnessed the safe descent of some over-daring aviator.

IV

As the train moved on, we six, who had been fellow-passengers for some thirty or forty minutes before the woman had entered our compartment, we who had not till then exchanged a word, broke suddenly into general conversation.

" Water on the brain; I don't care what any one says," asserted the rubicund man.

" My sister had one very similar," put in the failure, who was sitting next to me. " It died," he added, by way of giving point to his instance.

" Ought not to exhibit freaks like that in public," said an old man opposite to me.

" You're right, sir," was the verdict of the artisan, and he spat carefully and scraped his boot on the floor; " them things ought to be kep' private."

" Mad, of course, that's to say imbecile," repeated the rubicund man.

" Horrid head he'd got," said the failure, and shivered histrionically.

They continued to demonstrate their contempt for the infant by many asseverations. The reaction grew. They were all bold now, and all wanted to speak. They spoke as the survivors from some common peril; they were increasingly anxious to demonstrate that they had never suffered intimidation, and in their relief they were anxious to laugh at the thing which had for a time subdued them. But they never named it as a cause for fear. Their speech was merely innuendo.

At the last, however, I caught an echo of the true feeling.

It was the rubicund man who, most daring during the crisis, was now bold enough to admit curiosity.

"What's your opinion, sir?" he said to me. The train was running into Wenderby; he was preparing to get out; he leaned forward, his fingers on the handle of the door.

I was embarrassed. Why had I been singled out by the child? I had taken no part in the recent interjectory conversation. Was this a consequence of the notice that had been paid to me?

"I?" I stammered, and then reverted to the rubicund man's original phrase, "It—it was certainly a very remarkable child," I said.

The rubicund man nodded and pursed his lips. "Very," he muttered as he alighted, "Very remarkable. Well, good day to you."

I returned to my book, and was surprised to find that my index finger was still marking the place at which I had been interrupted some fifteen minutes before. My arm felt stiff and cramped.

I read " . . . this absence of any tangible reason is the more striking the deeper our freedom goes."

CHAPTER II

I

GINGER STOTT is a name that was once as well known as any in England. Stott has been the subject of leading articles in every daily paper ; his life has been written by an able journalist who interviewed Stott himself, during ten crowded minutes, and filled three hundred pages with details, seventy per cent. of which were taken from the journals, and the remainder supplied by a brilliant imagination. Ten years ago Ginger Stott was on a pinnacle, there was a Stott vogue. You found his name at the bottom of signed articles written by members of the editorial staff ; you bought Stott collars, although Stott himself did not wear collars ; there was a Stott waltz, which is occasionally hummed by clerks, and whistled by errand-boys to this day ; there was a periodical which lived for ten months, entitled *Ginger Stott's Weekly* ; in brief, during one summer there was a Stott apotheosis.

But that was ten years ago, and the rising generation has almost forgotten the once well-known name. One rarely sees him mentioned in the morning paper now, and then it is but the briefest reference; some such note as this "Pickering was at the top of his form, recalling the finest achievements of Ginger Stott at his best," or "Flack is a magnificent find for Kent: he promises to completely surpass the historic feats of Ginger Stott." These journalistic superlatives only irritate those who remember the performances referred to. We who watched the man's career know that Pickering and Flack are but tyros compared to Stott; we know that none of his successors has challenged comparison with him. He was a meteor that blazed across the sky, and if he ever has a true successor, such stars as Pickering and Flack will shine pale and dim in comparison.

It makes one feel suddenly old to recall that great matinée at the Lyceum, given for Ginger Stott's benefit after he met with his accident. In ten years so many great figures in that world have died or fallen into obscurity. I can count on my fingers the number of those who were then, and are still, in the forefront of popularity. Of the others poor Captain Wallis, for instance, is dead—and no modern writer, in my opinion, can equal the brilliant descriptiveness of Wallis's articles in the *Daily Post*. Bobby Maisefield, again, Stott's colleague, is a

martyr to rheumatism, and keeps a shop in Ailesworth, the scene of so many of his triumphs. What
a list one might make, but how uselessly. It is
enough to note how many names have dropped out,
how many others are the names of those we now
speak of as veterans. In ten years! It certainly
makes one feel old.

II

No apology is needed for telling again the story
of Stott's career. Certain details will still be
familiar, it is true, the historic details that can
never be forgotten while cricket holds place as
our national game. But there are many facts
of Stott's life familiar to me, which have never
been made public property. If I must repeat
that which is known, I can give the known a new
setting; perhaps a new value.

He came of mixed races. His mother was pure
Welsh, his father a Yorkshire collier; but when
Ginger was nine years old his father died, and
Mrs. Stott came to live in Ailesworth where she
had immigrant relations, and it was there that
she set up the little paper-shop, the business by
which she maintained herself and her boy. That
shop is still in existence, and the name has not
been altered. You may find it in the little street

that runs off the market place, going down towards the Borstal Institution.

There are many people alive in Ailesworth to-day who can remember the sturdy, freckled, sandy-haired boy who used to go round with the morning and evening papers; the boy who was to change the fortunes of a county.

Ginger was phenomenally thorough in all he undertook. It was one of the secrets of his success. It was this thoroughness that kept him engaged in his mother's little business until he was seventeen. Up to that age he never found time for cricket—he certainly had remarkable and very unusual qualities.

It was sheer chance, apparently, that determined his choice of a career.

He had walked into Stoke-Underhill to deliver a parcel, and on his way back his attention was arrested by the sight of a line of vehicles drawn up to the boarded fencing that encloses the Ailesworth County Ground. The occupants of these vehicles were standing up, struggling to catch a sight of the match that was being played behind the screen erected to shut out non-paying sight-seers. Among the horses' feet, squirming between the spokes of wheels, utterly regardless of all injury, small boys glued their eyes to knot-holes in the fence, while others climbed surreptitiously, and

2

for the most part unobserved, on to the backs of tradesmen's carts. All these individuals were in a state of tremendous excitement, and even the policeman whose duty it was to move them on, was so engrossed in watching the game that he had disappeared inside the turnstile, and had given the outside spectators full opportunity for eleemosynary enjoyment.

That tarred fence has since been raised some six feet, and now encloses a wider sweep of ground —alterations that may be classed among the minor revolutions effected by the genius of that thick-set, fair-haired youth of seventeen, who paused on that early September afternoon to wonder what all the fuss was about. The Ailesworth County Ground was not famous in those days; not then was accommodation needed for thirty thousand spectators, drawn from every county in England to witness the unparalleled.

Ginger stopped. The interest of the spectacle pierced his absorption in the business he had in hand. Such a thing was almost unprecedented.

" What's up ? " he asked of Puggy Phillips.

Puggy Phillips—hazarding his life by standing on the shiny, slightly curved top of his butcher's cart—made no appropriate answer. " Yah—*ah*—AH ! " he screamed in ecstasy. " Oh ! played ! Pla-a-a-ayed ! ! "

Ginger wasted no more breath, but laid hold of the little brass rail that encircled Puggy's platform, and with a sudden hoist that lifted the shafts and startled the pony, raised himself to the level of a spectator.

" 'Ere ! " shouted the swaying, tottering Puggy " What the . . . are yer rup to ? "

The well-drilled pony, however, settled down again quietly to maintain his end of the see-saw, and, finding himself still able to preserve his equilibrium, Puggy instantly forgot the presence of the intruder.

" What's up ? " asked Ginger again.

" Oh ! Well *'it,* WELL 'IT ! " yelled Puggy. " Oh ! Gow on, gow on agen ! Run it *aht.* Run it AH-T."

Ginger gave it up, and turned his attention to the match.

It was not any famous struggle that was being fought out on the old Ailesworth Ground ; it was only second-class cricket, the deciding match of the Minor Counties championship. Hampdenshire and Oxfordshire, old rivals, had been neck-and-neck all through the season, and, as luck would have it, the engagement between them had been the last fixture on the card.

When Ginger rose to the level of spectator, the match was anybody's game. Bobby Maisefield was batting. He was then a promising young colt who had not earned a fixed place in the Eleven. Ginger knew him socially, but they were not friends, they had no interests in common. Bobby had made twenty-seven. He was partnered by old Trigson, the bowler, (he has been dead these eight years,) whose characteristic score of "Not out . . . 0," is sufficiently representative of his methods.

It was the fourth innings, and Hampdenshire with only one more wicket to fall, still required nineteen runs to win. Trigson could be relied upon to keep his wicket up, but not to score. The hopes of Ailesworth centred in the ability of that almost untried colt Bobby Maisefield—and he seemed likely to justify the trust reposed in him. A beautiful late cut that eluded third man and hit the fence with a resounding bang, nearly drove Puggy wild with delight.

"Only fifteen more," he shouted. "Oh! Played; pla-a-a-yed!"

But as the score crept up, the tensity grew. As each ball was delivered, a chill, rigid silence held the onlookers in its grip. When Trigson, with the field collected round him, almost to be covered with a sheet, stonewalled the most tempting lob, the click of the ball on his bat was an intrusion on the stillness. And always it was followed by a deep breath of relief that sighed round the ring like a faint wind through a plantation of larches. When Bobby scored, the tumult broke out like a crash of thunder; but it subsided again, echoless, to that intense silence so soon as the ball was " dead."

Curiously, it was not Bobby who made the winning hit but Trigson. " One to tie, two to win," breathed Puggy as the field changed over, and it was Trigson who had to face the bowling. The suspense was torture. Oxford had put on their fast bowler again, and Trigson, intimidated, perhaps, did not play him with quite so straight a bat as he had opposed to the lob-bowler. The ball hit Trigson's bat and glanced through the slips. The field was very close to the wicket, and the ball was travelling fast. No one seemed to make any attempt to stop it. For a moment the significance of the thing was not realised; for a moment only, then followed uproar, deafening, stupendous.

Puggy was stamping fiercely on the top of his cart; the tears were streaming down his face; he was screaming and yelling incoherent words. He was representative of the crowd. Thus men shouted and stamped and cried when news came of the relief of Kimberley, or when that false report of victory was brought to Paris in the August of 1870. . . .

The effect upon Ginger was a thing apart. He did not join in the fierce acclamation; he did not wait to see the chairing of Bobby and Trigson. The greatness of Stott's character, the fineness of his genius is displayed in his attitude towards the dramatic spectacle he had just witnessed.

As he trudged home into Ailesworth, his thoughts found vent in a muttered sentence which is peculiarly typical of the effect that had been made upon him.

" I believe I could have bowled that chap," he said.

III

In writing a history of this kind, a certain licence must be claimed. It will be understood that I am filling certain gaps in the narrative with imagined detail. But the facts are true. My added detail is only intended to give an appearance of life and reality to my history. Let me, therefore, insist upon one vital point. I have not been dependent on hearsay for one single fact in this story Where my experience does not depend upon personal experience, it has been received from the principals themselves. Finally, it should be remembered that when I have, imaginatively, put words into the mouths of the persons of this story, they are never essential words which affect the issue. The essential speeches are reported from first-hand sources. For instance, Ginger Stott himself has told me on more than one occasion that the words

with which I closed the last section, were the
actual words spoken by him on the occasion in
question. It was not until six years after the
great Oxfordshire match that I myself first met
the man, but what follows is literally true in all
essentials.

There was a long, narrow strip of yard, or alley,
at the back of Mrs. Stott's paper-shop, a yard
that, unfortunately, no longer exists. It has
been partly built over, and another of England's
memorials has thus been destroyed by the vandals
of modern commerce. . . .

This yard was fifty-three feet long, measuring
from Mrs. Stott's back door to the door of the coal-
shed, which marked the alley's extreme limit. This
measurement, an apparently negligible trifle, had an
important effect upon Stott's career. For it was in
this yard that he taught himself to bowl, and the
shortness of the pitch precluded his taking any run.
From those long studious hours of practice he
emerged with a characteristic that was—and still
remains—unique. Stott never took more than two
steps before delivering the ball; frequently he
bowled from a standing position, and batsmen have
confessed that of all Stott's puzzling mannerisms,
this was the one to which they never became accustomed. S. R. L. Maturin, the finest bat Australia
ever sent to this country, has told me that to this

peculiarity of delivery he attributed his failure ever to score freely against Stott. It completely upset one's habit of play, he said: one had no time to prepare for the flight of the ball; it came at one so suddenly. Other bowlers have since attempted some imitation of this method without success. They had not Stott's physical advantages.

Nevertheless, the shortness of that alley threw Stott back for two years. When he first emerged to try conclusions on the field, he found his length on the longer pitch utterly unreliable, and the effort necessary to throw the ball another six yards, at first upset his slowly acquired methods.

It was not until he was twenty years old that Ginger Stott played in his first Colts' match.

The three years that had intervened had not been prosperous years for Hampdenshire. Their team was a one-man team. Bobby Maisefield was developing into a fine bat (and other counties were throwing out inducements to him, trying to persuade him to qualify for first-class cricket), but he found no support, and Hampdenshire was never looked upon as a coming county. The best of the minor counties in those years were Staffordshire and Norfolk.

In the Colts' match Stott's analysis ran:

overs	maidens	runs	wickets
11·3	7	16	7

and reference to the score-sheet, which is still preserved among the records of the County Club, shows that six of the seven wickets were clean bowled. The Eleven had no second innings ; the match was drawn, owing to rain. Stott has told me that the Eleven had to bat on a drying wicket, but after making all allowances, the performance was certainly phenomenal.

After this match Stott was, of course, played regularly. That year Hampdenshire rose once more to their old position at the head of the minor counties, and Maisefield, who had been seriously considering Surrey's offer of a place in their Eleven after two years' qualification by residence, decided to remain with the county which had given him his first chance.

During that season Stott did not record any performance so remarkable as his feat in the Colts' match, but his record for the year was eighty-seven wickets with an average of 9˙31 ; and it is worthy of notice that Yorkshire made overtures to him, as he was qualified by birth to play for the northern county.

I think there must have been a wonderful *esprit de corps* among the members of that early Hampden-shire Eleven. There are other evidences beside this refusal of its two most prominent members to join the ranks of first-class cricket. Lord R——, the president of the H.C.C.C., has told me that this spirit was quite as marked as in the earlier case of Kent. He himself certainly did much to promote it, and his generosity in making good the deficits of the balance sheet, had a great influence on the acceleration of Hampdenshire's triumph.

In his second year, though Hampdenshire were again champions of the second-class counties, Stott had not such a fine average as in the preceding season. Sixty-one wickets for eight hundred and sixty-eight (average 14·23) seems to show a decline in his powers, but that was a wonderful year for batsmen (Maisefield scored seven hundred and forty-two runs, with an average of forty-two) and, moreover, that was the year in which Stott was privately practising his new theory.

It was in this year that three very promising recruits, all since become famous, joined the Eleven, viz. : P. H. Evans, St. John Townley, and Flower the fast bowler. With these five cricketers Hampdenshire fully deserved their elevation into the list of first-class counties. Curiously enough, they took the place of the old champions, Gloucestershire, who, with Somerset, fell back into the obscurity of the second-class that season.

IV

I must turn aside for a moment at this point in order to explain the " new theory " of Stott's, to which I have referred, a theory which became in practice one of the elements of his most astounding successes.

Ginger Stott was not a tall man. He stood only 5 ft. 5¼ in. in his socks, but he was tremendously solid ; he had what is known as a " stocky " figure, broad and deep-chested. That was where his muscular power lay, for his abnormally long arms were rather thin, though his huge hands were powerful enough.

Even without his " new theory," Stott would have been an exceptional bowler. His thoroughness would have assured his success. He studied his art diligently, and practised regularly in a barn through the winter. His physique, too, was a magnificent instrument. That long, muscular body was superbly steady on the short, thick legs. It gave him a fulcrum, firm, apparently immovable. And those weirdly long, thin arms could move with lightning rapidity. He always stood with his hands behind him, and then—as often as not without even one preliminary step—the long arm would flash round and the ball be delivered, without giving the batsman any opportunity of watching his hand ; you could never tell which way he was going to break. It was astonishing, too, the pace he could get without any run. Poor Wallis used to call him the "human catapult"; Wallis was always trying to find new phrases.

The theory first came to Stott when he was practising at the nets. It was a windy morning, and he noticed that several times the balls he bowled swerved in the air. When those swerving balls came they were almost unplayable.

Stott made no remark to any one—he was bowling to the groundsman—but the ambition to bowl "swerves," as they were afterwards called, took possession of him from that morning. It is true that he never mastered the theory completely; on a perfectly calm day he could never depend upon obtaining any swerve at all, but, within limits, he developed his theory until he had any batsman practically at his mercy.

He might have mastered the theory completely, had it not been for his accident—we must remember that he had only three seasons of first-class cricket— and, personally, I believe he would have achieved that complete mastery. But I do not believe, as Stott did, that he could have taught his method to another man. That belief became an obsession with him, and will be dealt with later.

My own reasons for doubting that Stott's

" swerve " could have been taught, is that it would have been necessary for the pupil to have had Stott's peculiarities, not only of method, but of physique. He used to spin the ball with a twist of his middle finger and thumb, just as you may see a billiard professional spin a billiard ball. To do this in his manner, it is absolutely necessary not only to have a very large and muscular hand, but to have very lithe and flexible arm muscles, for the arm is moving rapidly while the twist is given, and there must be no antagonistic muscular action. Further, I believe that part of the secret was due to the fact that Stott bowled from a standing position. Given these things, the rest is merely a question of long and assiduous practice. The human mechanism is marvellously adaptable. I have seen Stott throw a cricket ball half across the room with sufficient spin on the ball to make it shoot back to him along the carpet.

I have mentioned the wind as a factor in obtaining the swerve. It was a head-wind that Stott required. I have seen him, for sport, toss a cricket ball into the teeth of a gale, and make it describe the trajectory of a badly sliced golf-ball. This is why the big pavilion at Ailesworth is set at such a curious angle to the ground. It was built in the winter following Hampdenshire's second season of first-class cricket, and it was so placed that when the wickets were pitched in a line with it, they might lie south-west and north-east, or in the direction of the prevailing winds.

v

The first time I ever saw Ginger Stott, was on the occasion of the historic encounter with Surrey; Hampdenshire's second engagement in first-class cricket. The match with Notts, played at Trent Bridge a few days earlier, had not foreshadowed any startling results. The truth of the matter is that Stott had been kept, deliberately, in the background; and as matters turned out his services were only required to finish off Notts' second innings. Stott was even then a marked man, and the Hampdenshire captain did not wish to advertise his methods too freely before the Surrey match. Neither Archie Findlater, who was captaining the team that year, nor any other person, had the least conception of how unnecessary such a reservation was to prove. In his third year, when Stott had been studied by every English, Australian, and South African batsman of any note, he was still as unplayable as when he made his début in first-class cricket.

I was reporting the Surrey match for two papers, and in company with poor Wallis interviewed Stott before the first innings.

His appearance made a great impression on me.

I have, of course, met him, and talked with him many times since then, but my most vivid memory of him is the picture recorded in the inadequate professional dressing-room of the old Ailesworth pavilion.

I have turned up the account of my interview in an old press-cutting book, and I do not know that I can do better than quote that part of it which describes Stott's personal appearance. I wrote the account on the off chance of being able to get it taken. It was one of my lucky hits. After that match, finished in a single day, my interview afforded copy that any paper would have paid heavily for, and gladly.

Here is the description :

" Stott—he is known to every one in Ailesworth as ' Ginger ' Stott—is a short, thick-set young man, with abnormally long arms that are tanned a rich red up to the elbow. The tan does not, however, obliterate the golden freckles with which arm and face are richly speckled. There is no need to speculate as to the *raison d'être* of his nickname. The hair of his head, a close, short crop, is a pale russet, and the hair on his hands and arms is a yellower shade of the same colour. ' Ginger ' is, indeed, a perfectly apt description. He has a square chin and a thin-lipped, determined mouth. His eyes are a clear, but rather light blue, his forehead is good, broad, and high, and he has a well-proportioned head. One might have put him down as an engineer, essentially intelligent, purposeful, and reserved."

The description is journalistic, but I do not know that I could improve upon the detail of it. I can see those queer, freckled, hairy arms of his as I write—the combination of colours in them produced an effect that was almost orange. It struck one as unusual. . . .

Surrey had the choice of innings, and decided to bat, despite the fact that the wicket was drying after rain, under the influence of a steady south-west wind and occasional bursts of sunshine. Would any captain in Stott's second year have dared to take first innings under such conditions ? The question is farcical now, but not a single 'member of the Hampdenshire Eleven had the least conception that the Surrey captain was deliberately throwing away his chances on that eventful day.

Wallis and I were sitting together in the reporters' box. There were only four of us ; two specials,— Wallis and myself,—a news-agency reporter, and a local man.

"Stott takes first over," remarked Wallis, sharpening his pencil and arranging his watch and score-sheet—he was very meticulous in his methods. " They've put him to bowl against the wind. He's medium right, isn't he ? "

" Haven't the least idea," I said. " He volunteered no information; Hampdenshire have been keeping him dark."

Wallis sneered. " Think they've got a find, eh ? " he said. " We'll wait and see what he can do against first-class batting."

We did not have to wait long.

As usual, Thorpe and Harrison were first wicket for Surrey, and Thorpe took the first ball.

It bowled him. It made his wicket look as untidy as any wicket I have ever seen. The off stump was out of the ground, and the other two were markedly divergent.

" Damn it, I wasn't ready for him," we heard Thorpe say in the professionals' room. Thorpe always had some excuse, but on this occasion it was justified.

C. V. Punshon was the next comer, and he got his first ball through the slips for four, but Wallis looked at me with a raised eyebrow.

" Punshon didn't know a lot about that," he said, and then he added, " I say, what a queer delivery the chap has. He stands and shoots 'em out. It's uncanny. He's a kind of human catapult." He made a note of the phrase on his pad.

Punshon succeeded in hitting the next ball, also, but it simply ran up his bat into the hands of short slip.

" Well, that's a sitter, if you like," said Wallis. " What's the matter with 'em ? "

3

I was beginning to grow enthusiastic.

" Look here, Wallis," I said, " this chap's going to break records."

Wallis was still doubtful.

He was convinced before the innings was over.

There must be many who remember the startling poster that heralded the early editions of the evening papers :

SURREY

ALL OUT

FOR 13 RUNS.

For once sub-editors did not hesitate to give the score on the contents bill.   That was a proclamation which would sell.   Inside, the headlines were rich and varied.   I have an old paper by me, yellow now, and brittle, that may serve as a type for the rest. The headlines are as follows :—

SURREY AND HAMPDENSHIRE.

———

EXTRAORDINARY BOWLING
PERFORMANCE.

———

DOUBLE HAT-TRICK.

———

SURREY ALL OUT IN 35 MINUTES
FOR 13 RUNS.

———

STOTT TAKES 10 WICKETS FOR 5.

The " double hat-trick " was six consecutive wickets, the last six, all clean bowled.

" Good God ! " Wallis said, when the last wicket fell, and he looked at me with something like fear in his eyes. " This man will have to be barred; it means the end of cricket."

I need not detail the remainder of the match. Hampdenshire hit up ninety-three—P. H. Evans was top scorer with twenty-seven—and then got Surrey out a second time for forty-nine.

I believe Stott did not bowl his best in the second innings. He was quite clever enough to see that he must not overdo it. As Wallis had said, if he were too effective he might have to be barred. As it was, he took seven wickets for twenty-three.

VI

That was Stott's finest performance. On eight subsequent occasions he took all ten wickets in a single innings, once he took nineteen wickets in one match (Hampdenshire v. Somerset at Taunton), twice he took five wickets with consecutive balls, and any number of times he did the " hat-trick," but he never afterwards achieved so amazing a performance as that of the celebrated Surrey match.

I am still of opinion that Stott deliberately bowled carelessly in the second innings of that match, but, after watching him on many fields, and after a careful analysis of his methods—and character—I am quite certain that his comparative failures in later matches were not due to any purpose on Stott's part.

Take, for instance, the match which Hampdenshire lost to Kent in Stott's second season—their first loss as a first-class county; their record up to that time was thirteen wins and six drawn games. It is incredible to me that Stott should have deliberately allowed Kent to make the necessary one hundred and eighty-seven runs required in the fourth innings. He took five wickets for sixty-three; if he could have done better, I am sure he would have made the effort. He would not have sacrificed his county. I have spoken of the *esprit de corps* which held the Hampdenshire Eleven together, and they were notably proud of their unbeaten record.

No; we must find another reason for Stott's comparative failures. I believe that I am the only person who knows that reason, and I say that Stott was the victim of an obsession. His "swerve" theory dominated him, he was always experimenting with it, and when, as in the Kent match I have cited, the game was played in a flat calm, his failure to influence the trajectory of the ball in his own peculiar manner, puzzled and upset him. He would strive to make the ball swerve, and in the effort he lost his length and became playable. Moreover, when Stott was hit he lost his temper, and then he was useless. Findlater always took him off the moment he showed signs of temper. The usual sign was a fast full pitch at the batsman's ribs.

I have one more piece of evidence, the best possible, which upholds this explanation of mine, but it must follow the account of Stott's accident.

That accident came during the high flood of Hampdenshire success. For two years they had held undisputed place as champion county, a place which could not be upset by the most ingenious methods of calculating points. They had three times defeated Australia, and were playing four men in the test matches. As a team they were capable of beating any Eleven opposed to them. Not even the newspaper critics denied that.

In this third year of Hampdenshire's triumph, Australia had sent over the finest eleven that had ever represented the colony, but they had lost the first two test matches, and they had lost to Hampdenshire. Nevertheless, they won the rubber, and took back the " ashes." No one has ever denied, I believe, that this was due to Stott's accident. There is in this case no room for any one to argue that the argument is based on the fallacy of *post* and *propter*.

The accident appeared insignificant at the time.

The match was against Notts on the Trent Bridge ground. I was reporting for three papers ; Wallis was not there.

Stott had been taken off. Notts were a poor lot that year and I think Findlater did not wish to make their defeat appear too ignominious. Flower was bowling ; it was a fast, true wicket, and Stott, who was a safe field, was at cover.

G. L. Mallinson was batting and making good use of his opportunity ; he was, it will be remembered, a magnificent though erratic hitter. Flower bowled him a short-pitched, fast ball, rather wide of the off-stump. Many men might have left it alone, for the ball was rising, and the slips were crowded, but Mallinson timed the ball splendidly, and drove it with all his force. He could not keep it on the ground, however, and Stott had a possible chance. He leaped for it and just touched the ball with his right hand. The ball jumped the ring at its first bound, and Mallinson never even attempted to run. There was a big round of applause from the Trent Bridge crowd.

I noticed that Stott had tied a handkerchief round his finger, but I forgot the incident until I saw Findlater beckon to his best bowler, a few overs later. Notts had made enough runs for decency ; it was time to get them out.

I saw Stott walk up to Findlater and shake his

head, and through my glasses I saw him whip the handkerchief from his finger and display his hand. Findlater frowned, said something and looked towards the pavilion, but Stott shook his head. He evidently disagreed with Findlater's proposal. Then Mallinson came up, and the great bulk of his back hid the faces of the other two. The crowd was beginning to grow excited at the interruption. Every one had guessed that something was wrong. All round the ring men were standing up, trying to make out what was going on.

I drew my inferences from Mallinson's face, for when he turned round and strolled back to his wicket, he was wearing a broad smile. Through my field glasses I could see that he was licking his lower lip with his tongue. His shoulders were humped and his whole expression one of barely controlled glee. (I always see that picture framed in a circle ; a bioscopic presentation.) He could hardly refrain from dancing. Then little Beale, who was Mallinson's partner, came up and spoke to him, and I saw Mallinson hug himself with delight as he explained the situation.

When Stott unwillingly came into the pavilion, a low murmur ran round the ring, like the buzz of a great crowd of disturbed blue flies. In that murmur I could distinctly trace the signs of mixed feelings. No doubt the crowd had come there to witness the

performances of the phenomenon—the abnormal of
every kind has a wonderful attraction for us—but,
on the other hand, the majority wanted to see their
own county win. Moreover, Mallinson was giving
them a taste of his abnormal powers of hitting, and
the batsman appeals to the spectacular, more than
the bowler.

I ran down hurriedly to meet Stott.

"Only a split finger, sir," he said carelessly, in
answer to my question; "but Mr. Findlater says I
must see to it."

I examined the finger, and it certainly did not
seem to call for surgical aid. Evidently it had been
caught by the seam of the new ball; there was a
fairly clean cut about half an inch long on the fleshy
underside of the second joint of the middle finger.

"Better have it seen to," I said. "We can't
afford to lose you, you know, Stott."

Stott gave a laugh that was more nearly a snarl.
"Ain't the first time I've 'ad a cut finger," he said
scornfully.

He had the finger bound up when I saw him again,
but it had been done by an amateur. I learnt afterwards that no antiseptic had been used. That was
at lunch time, and Notts had made a hundred and
sixty-eight for one wicket; Mallinson was not out,
a hundred and three. I saw that the Notts
Eleven were in magnificent spirits.

But after lunch Stott came out and took the first over. I don't know what had passed between him and Findlater, but the captain had evidently been over-persuaded.

We must not blame Findlater. The cut certainly appeared trifling, it was not bad enough to prevent Stott from bowling, and Hampdenshire seemed powerless on that wicket without him. It is very easy to distribute blame after the event, but most people would have done what Findlater did in those circumstances.

The cut did not appear to inconvenience Stott in the least degree. He bowled Mallinson with his second ball, and the innings was finished up in another fifty-seven minutes for the addition of thirty-eight runs.

Hampdenshire made two hundred and thirty-seven for three wickets before the drawing of stumps, and that was the end of the match, for the weather changed during the night and rain prevented any further play.

I, of course, stayed on in Nottingham to await results. I saw Stott on the next day, Friday, and asked him about his finger. He made light of it, but that evening Findlater told me over the bridge-table that he was not happy about it. He had seen the finger, and thought it showed a tendency to inflammation. " I shall take him to Gregory in the

morning if it's not all right," he said. Gregory was
a well-known surgeon in Nottingham.

Again one sees, now, that the visit to Gregory
should not have been postponed, but at the time one
does not take extraordinary precautions in such a
case as this. A split finger is such an everyday
thing, and one is guided by the average of experience.
After all, if one were constantly to make preparation
for the abnormal, ordinary life could not go on. . . .

I heard that Gregory pursed his lips over that
finger when he had learned the name of his famous
patient. " You'll have to be very careful of this,
young man," was Findlater's report of Gregory's
advice. It was not sufficient. I often wonder now
whether Gregory might not have saved the finger.
If he had performed some small operation at once,
cut away the poison, it seems to me that the tragedy
might have been averted. I am, I admit, a mere
layman in these matters, but it seems to me that
something might have been done.

I left Nottingham on Saturday after lunch—the
weather was hopeless—and I did not make use of
the information I had for the purposes of my paper.
I was never a good journalist. But I went down to
Ailesworth on Monday morning, and found that
Findlater and Stott had already gone to Harley
Street to see Graves, the King's surgeon.

I followed them, and arrived at Graves's house

while Stott was in the consulting-room.   I hocussed
the butler and waited with the patients.   Among
the papers, I came upon the famous caricature of
Stott in the current number of *Punch*—the " Stand-
and-Deliver" caricature, in which Stott is represented
with an arm about ten feet long, and the batsman
is looking wildly over his shoulder to square leg,
bewildered, with no conception from what direction
the ball is coming.   Underneath is written " Stott's
New Theory—the Ricochet.   Real Ginger."   While
I was laughing over the cartoon, the butler came in
and nodded to me.   I followed him out of the room
and met Findlater and Stott in the hall.

Findlater was in a state of profanity.   I could not
get a sensible word out of him.   He was in a white
heat of pure rage.   The butler, who seemed as
anxious as I to learn the verdict, was positively
frightened.

" Well, for God's sake tell me what Graves said,"
I protested.

Findlater's answer is unprintable, and told me
nothing.

Stott, however, quite calm and self-possessed,
volunteered the information.   " Finger's got to
come off, sir," he said quietly.   " Doctor says if it
ain't off to-day or to-morrer, he won't answer for
my 'and."

This was the news I had to give to England.   It

was a great coup from the journalistic point of view, but I made up my three columns with a heavy heart, and the congratulations of my editor only sickened me. I had some luck, but I should never have become a good journalist.

The operation was performed successfully that evening, and Stott's career was closed.

VII

I have already referred to the obsession which dominated Stott after his accident, and I must now deal with that overweening anxiety of his to teach his method to another man.

I did not see Stott again till August, and then I had a long talk with him on the Ailesworth County Ground, as together we watched the progress of Hampdenshire's defeat by Lancashire.

"Oh! I can't learn him *nothing*," he broke out, as Flower was hit to the four corners of the ground, "'alf vollies and long 'ops and then a full pitch—'e's a disgrace."

"They've knocked him off his length," I protested. "On a wicket like this . . ."

Stott shook his head. "I've been trying to learn 'im," he said, "but he can't never learn. 'E's got 'abits what you can't break 'im of."

"I suppose it *is* difficult," I said vaguely.

"Same with me," went on Stott, "I've been

trying to learn myself to bowl without my finger "—
he held up his mutilated hand—" or left-'anded ;
but I can't.   If I'd started that way . . . No ! I'm
always feeling for that finger as is gone.   A second-
class bowler I might be in time, not better nor
that."

" It's early days yet," I ventured, intending encouragement, but Stott frowned and shook his head.

" I'm not going to kid myself," he said, " I know.
But I'm going to find a youngster and learn 'im.
On'y he must be young."

" No 'abits, you know," he explained.

The next time I met Stott was in November.   I
ran up against him, literally, one Friday afternoon
in Ailesworth.

When he recognised me he asked me if I would
care to walk out to Stoke-Underhill with him.   " I've
took a cottage there," he explained, " I'm to be
married in a fortnight's time."

His circumstances certainly warranted such a venture.   The proceeds of matinée and benefit, invested
for him by the Committee of the County Club, produced an income of nearly two pounds a week, and
in addition to this he had his salary as groundsman.
I tendered my congratulations.

" Oh ! well, as to that, better wait a bit," said
Stott.

He walked with his hands in his pockets and his

eyes on the ground. He had the air of a man brooding over some project.

" It *is* a lottery, of course . . . " I began, but he interrupted me.

" Oh that ! " he said, and kicked a stone into the ditch ; " take my chances of that. It's the kid I'm thinking on."

" The kid ? " I repeated, doubtful whether he spoke of his fiancée, or whether his nuptials pointed an act of reparation.

" What else 'ud I tie myself up for ? " asked Stott. " I must 'ave a kid of my own and learn 'im from his cradle. It's come to that."

" Oh ! I understand," I said ; " teach him to bowl."

" Ah ! " replied Stott as an affirmative. " Learn 'im to bowl from his cradle ; before 'e's got 'abits. When I started I'd never bowled a ball in my life, and by good luck I started right. But I can't find another kid over seven years old in England as ain't never bowled a ball o' some sort and started 'abits. I've tried . . . "

" And you hope with your own boys . . . ? " I said.

" Not 'ope, it's a cert ; " said Stott. " I'll see no boy of mine touches a ball afore he's fourteen, and then 'e'll learn from me ; and learn right. From the first go off." He was silent for a few seconds, and then he broke out in a kind of ecstasy. "My Gawd, 'e'll be a bowler such as 'as never been, never in this world. He'll start where I left orf. He'll . . . " Words failed him, he fell back on the expletive he had used, repeating it with an awed fervour. "My Gawd!"

I had never seen Stott in this mood before. It was a revelation to me of the latent potentialities of the man, the remarkable depth and quality of his ambitions. . . .

VIII

I intended to be present at Stott's wedding, but I was not in England when it took place ; indeed, for the next two years and a half I was never in England for more than a few days at a time. I sent him a wedding-present, an inkstand in the guise of a cricket ball, with a pen-rack that was built of little silver wickets. They were still advertised that Christmas as "Stott inkstands."

Two years and a half of American life broke up many of my old habits of thought. When I first returned to London I found that the cricket news no longer held the same interest for me, and this may account for the fact that I did not trouble for some time to look up my old friend Stott.

In July, however, affairs took me to Ailesworth, and the associations of the place naturally led me to wonder how Stott's marriage had turned out, and whether the much-desired son had been born to him. When my business in Ailesworth was done, I decided to walk out to Stoke-Underhill.

The road passes the County Ground, and a match was in progress, but I walked by without stopping. I was wool-gathering. I was not thinking of the man I was going to see, or I should have turned in at the County Ground, where he would inevitably have been found. Instead, I was thinking of the abnormal child I had seen in the train that day; uselessly speculating and wondering.

When I reached Stoke-Underhill I found the cottage which Stott had shown me. I had by then so far recovered my wits as to know that I should not find Stott himself there, but from the look of the cottage I judged that it was untenanted, so I made inquiries at the post-office.

" No; he don't live here, now, sir," said the postmistress; " he lives at Pym, now, sir, and rides into Ailesworth on his bike." She was evidently about to furnish me with other particulars, but I did not care to hear them. I was moody and distrait. I was wondering why I should bother my head about so insignificant a person as this Stott.

" You'll be sure to find Mr. Stott at the cricket ground," the postmistress called after me.

Another two months of English life induced a

return to my old habits of thought. I found myself reverting to old tastes and interests. The reversion was a pleasant one. In the States I had been forced out of my groove, compelled to work, to strive, to think desperately if I would maintain any standing among my contemporaries. But when the perpetual stimulus was removed, I soon fell back to the less strenuous methods of my own country. I had time, once more, for the calm reflection that is so unlike the urgent, forced, inventive thought of the American journalist. I was braced by that thirty months' experience, perhaps hardened a little, but by September my American life was fading into the background; I had begun to take an interest in cricket again.

With the revival of my old interests, revived also my curiosity as to Ginger Stott, and one Sunday in late September I decided to go down to Pym.

It was a perfect day, and I thoroughly enjoyed my four-mile walk from Great Hittenden Station.

Pym is a tiny hamlet made up of three farms and a dozen scattered cottages. Perched on one of the highest summits of the Hampden Hills and lost in the thick cover of beech woods, without a post-office or a shop, Pym is the most perfectly isolated village within a reasonable distance of London. As I sauntered up the mile-long lane that climbs the steep hill, and is the only connection between Pym

4

and anything approaching a decent road, I thought
that this was the place to which I should like to
retire for a year, in order to write the book I had so
often contemplated, and never found time to begin.
This, I reflected, was a place of peace, of freedom
from all distraction, the place for calm, contem-
plative meditation.

I met no one in the lane, and there was no sign of
life when I reached what I must call the village,
though the word conveys a wrong idea, for there is
no street, merely a cottage here and there, dropped
haphazard, and situated without regard to its
aspect. These cottages lie all on one's left hand ;
to the right a stretch of grass soon merges into
bracken and bush, and then the beech woods enclose
both, and surge down into the valley and rise up
again beyond, a great wave of green ; as I saw it then,
not yet touched with the first flame of autumn.

I inquired at the first cottage and received my
direction to Stott's dwelling. It lay up a little lane,
the further of two cottages joined together.

The door stood open, and after a moment's hesitation and a light knock, I peered in.

Sitting in a rocking-chair was a woman with black,
untidy eyebrows, and on her knee, held with rigid
attention, was the remarkable baby I had seen in
the train two months before. As I stood, doubtful
and, I will confess it, intimidated, suddenly cold and

nervous, the child opened his eyes and honoured me with a cold stare. Then he nodded, a reflective, recognisable nod.

" 'E remembers seein' you in the train, sir," said the woman, " 'e never forgets any one. Did you want to see my 'usband ? 'E's upstairs."

So *this* was the boy who was designed by Stott to become the greatest bowler the world had ever seen. . . .

CHAPTER III

THE DISILLUSIONMENT OF GINGER STOTT

I

STOTT maintained an obstinate silence as we walked together up to the Common, a stretch of comparatively open ground on the plateau of the hill. He walked with his hands in his pockets and his head down, as he had walked out from Ailesworth with me nearly three years before, but his mood was changed. I was conscious that he was gloomy, depressed, perhaps a little unstrung. I was burning with curiosity. Now that I was released from the thrall of the child's presence, I was eager to hear all there was to tell of its history.

Presently we sat down under an ash-tree, one of three that guarded a shallow, muddy pond skimmed with weed. Stott accepted my offer of a cigarette, but seemed disinclined to break the silence.

I found nothing better to say than a repetition of the old phrase. "That's a very remarkable baby of yours, Stott," I said.

"Ah!" he replied, his usual substitute for

" yes," and he picked up a piece of dead wood and threw it into the little pond.

" How old is he ? " I asked.

" Nearly two year."

" Can he . . . " I paused ; my imagination was reconstructing the scene of the railway carriage, and I felt a reflex of the hesitation shown by the rubicund man when he had asked the same question. " Can he . . . can he talk ? " It seemed so absurd a question to ask, yet it was essentially a natural question in the circumstances.

" He can, but he won't."

This was startling enough, and I pressed my enquiry.

" How do you know ? Are you sure he can ? "

" Ah ! " Only that aggravating, monosyllabic assent.

" Look here, Stott," I said, " don't you want to talk about the child ? "

He shrugged his shoulders and threw more wood into the pond with a strained attentiveness as though he were peculiarly anxious to hit some particular wafer of the vivid, floating weed. For a full five minutes we maintained silence. I was trying to subdue my impatience and my temper. I knew Stott well enough to know that if I displayed signs of either, I should get no information from him. My self-control was rewarded at last.

" I've 'eard 'im speak," he said, " speak proper,
too, not like a baby."

He paused, and I grunted to show that I was
listening, but as he volunteered no further remark,
I said : " What did you hear him say ? "

" I dunno," replied Stott, " somethin' about
learnin' and talkin'. I didn't get the rights of it,
but the missus near fainted—*she* thinks 'e's Gawd
A'mighty or suthing."

" But why don't you make him speak ? " I asked
deliberately.

" Make 'im ! " said Stott, with a curl of his lip,
" *make* 'im ! You try it on ! "

I knew I was acting a part, but I wanted to pro-
voke more information. " Well ! Why not ? " I
said.

" 'Cos 'e'd look at you—that's why not," replied
Stott, " and you can't no more face 'im than a dog
can face a man. I shan't stand it much longer."

" Curious," I said, " very curious."

" Oh ! he's a blarsted freak, that's what 'e is,"
said Stott, getting to his feet and beginning to pace
moodily up and down.

I did not interrupt him. I was thinking of this
man who had drawn huge crowds from every part
of England, who had been a national hero, and who,
now, was unable to face his own child. Presently
Stott broke out again.

" To think of all the trouble I took when 'e was comin'," he said, stopping in front of me. " There was nothin' the missus fancied as I wouldn't get. We was livin' in Stoke then." He made a movement of his head in the direction of Ailesworth. " Not as she was difficult," he went on thoughtfully. " She used to say ' I mussent get 'abits, George.' Caught that from me ; I was always on about that —then. You know, thinkin' of learnin' 'im bowlin'. Things was different then ; afore 'e came." He paused again, evidently thinking of his troubles.

Sympathetically, I was wondering how far the child had separated husband and wife. There was the making of a tragedy here, I thought ; but when Stott, after another period of pacing up and down, began to speak again I found that his tragedy was of another kind.

" Learn '*im* bowling ! " he said, and laughed a mirthless laugh. " My Gawd ! it 'ud take something. No fear ; that little game's off. And I could a' done it if he'd been a decent or'nery child, 'stead of a blarsted freak. There won't never be another, neither. This one pretty near killed the missus. Doctor said it'd be 'er last. . . . With an 'ead like that, whacher expect ? "

" Can he walk ? " I asked.

" Ah ! Gets about easy enough for all 'is body and legs is so small. When the missus tries to stop 'im—she's afraid 'e'll go over—'e just looks at 'er and she 'as to let 'im 'ave 'is own way."

Later, I reverted to that speech of the child's, that intelligent, illuminating speech that seemed to prove that there was indeed a powerful, thoughtful mind behind those profoundly speculative eyes.

" That time he spoke, Stott," I said, " was he alone ? "

" Ah ! " assented Stott. " In the garden, practisin' walkin' all by 'imself."

" Was that the only time ? "

" Only time *I've* 'eard 'im."

" Was it lately ? "

" 'Bout six weeks ago."

" And he has never made a sound otherwise, cried, laughed ? "

" 'Ardly. 'E gives a sort o' grunt sometimes, when e' wants anything—and points."

" He's very intelligent."

" Worse than that, 'e's a freak, I tell you."

With the repetition of this damning description, Stott fell back into his moody pacing, and this time I failed to rouse him from his gloom. " Oh ! forget it," he broke out once, when I asked him another question, and I saw that he was not likely to give me any more information that day.

We walked back together, and I said good-bye to him at the end of the lane which led up to his cottage.

"Not comin' up ?" he asked, with a nod of his head towards his home.

"Well! I have to catch that train . . . " I prevaricated, looking at my watch. I did not wish to see that child again ; my distaste was even stronger than my curiosity.

Stott grinned. "We don't 'ave many visitors," he said. "Well, I'll come a bit farther with you."

He came to the bottom of the hill, and after he left me he took the road that goes over the hill to Wenderby. It would be about seven miles back to Pym by that road. . . .

III

I spent the next afternoon in the Reading Room of the British Museum. I was searching for a precedent, and at last I found one in the story of Christian Heinrich Heinecken,* who was born at Lubeck on February 6, 1721. There were marked points of difference between the development of Heinecken and that of Stott's child. Heinecken was physically feeble; at the age of three he was still being fed at the breast. The Stott precocity

---

* See the Teutsche Bibliothek and Schoneich's account of the child of Lubeck.

appeared to be physically strong ; his body looked
small and undeveloped, it is true, but this was partly
an illusion produced by the abnormal size of the
head.   Again Heinecken learned to speak very early ;
at ten months old he was asking intelligent questions,
at eighteen months he was studying history, geo-
graphy, Latin and anatomy ; whereas the Stott
child had only once been heard to speak at the age
of two years, and had not, apparently, begun any
study at all.

From this comparison it might seem at first that
the balance of precocity lay in the Heinecken scale.
I drew another inference.   I argued that the genius
of the Stott child far outweighed the genius of Christian Heinecken.

Little Heinecken in his four years of life suffered
the mental experience—with certain necessary limitations—of a developed brain.   He gathered knowledge as an ordinary child gathers knowledge, the
only difference being that his rate of assimilation
was as ten to one.

But little Stott had gathered no knowledge from
books.   He had been born of ignorant parents, he
was being brought up among uneducated people.
Yet he had wonderful intellectual gifts : surely he
must have one above all others—the gift of reason.
His brain must be constructive, logical ; he must
have the power of deduction.   He must even at an

extraordinarily early age, say six months, have developed some theory of life. He must be withholding his energy, deliberately; declining to exhibit his powers, holding his marvellous faculties in reserve. Here was surely a case of genius which, comparable in some respects to the genius of Heinecken, yet far exceeded it.

As I developed my theory, my eagerness grew. And then suddenly an inspiration came to me. In my excitement I spoke aloud and smacked the desk in front of me with my open hand. "Why, of course!" I said. "That is the key."

An old man in the next seat scowled fiercely. The attendants in the central circular desk all looked up. Other readers turned round and stared at me. I had violated the sacred laws of the Reading Room. I saw one of the librarians make a sign to an attendant and point to me.

I gathered up my books quickly and returned them at the central desk. My self-consciousness had returned, and I was anxious to be away from the observation of the many dilettante readers who found my appearance more engrossing than the books with which they were dallying on some pretext or another.

Yet, curiously, when I reached the street, the theory which had come to me in the Museum with the force and vividness of an illuminating dream had lost some of its glamour. Nevertheless, I set it out as it then shaped itself in my mind.

The great restraining force in the evolution of man, so I thought, has been the restriction imposed by habit. What we call instinct is a hereditary habit. This is the first guiding principle in the life of the human infant. Upon this instinct we immediately superimpose the habits of reason, all the bodily and intellectual conventions that have been handed down from generation to generation. We learn everything we know as children by the hereditary, simian habit of imitation. The child of intellectual, cultured parents, born into savage surroundings, becomes the slave of this inherited habit—call it tendency, if you will, the intention is the same. I elaborated the theory by instance and introspection, and found no flaw in it. . . .

And here, by some freak of nature, was a child born without these habits. During the period of gestation, one thought had dominated the minds of both parents—the desire to have a son born without habits. It does not seriously affect the theory that the desire had a peculiar end in view ; the wish, the urgent, controlling, omnipotent will had been there, and the result included far more than the specific intention.

Already some of my distaste for the Stott child had vanished. It was accountable, and therefore

no longer fearful. The child was supernormal, a
cause of fear to the normal man, as all truly supernormal things are to our primitive, animal instincts.
This is the fear of the wild thing ; when we can
explain and give reasons, the horror vanishes. We
are men again.

I did not quite recover the glow of my first inspiration, but the theory remained with me ; I decided to make a study of the child, to submit
knowledge to his reason. I would stand between
him and the delimiting training of the pedagogue, I
thought.

Then I reached home, and my life was changed.

This story is not of my own life, and I have no
wish to enter into the curious and saddening experiences which stood between me and the child of
Ginger Stott for nearly six years. In that time my
thoughts strayed now and again to that cottage in
the little hamlet on those wooded hills. Often I
thought " When I have time I will go and see that
child again if he is alive." But as the years passed,
the memory of him grew dim, even the memory of
his father was blurred over by a thousand new im-
pressions. So it chanced that for nearly six years
I heard no word of Stott and his supernormal infant,
and then chance again intervened. My long period
of sorrow came to an end almost as suddenly as
it had begun, and by a coincidence I was once

more entangled in the strange web of the phenomenal.

In this story of Victor Stott I have bridged these
six years in the pages that follow. In doing this I
have been compelled to draw to a certain extent on
my imagination, but the main facts are true. They
have been gathered from first-hand authority only,
from Henty Challis, from Mrs. Stott, and from her
husband ; though none, I must confess, has been
checked by that soundest of all authorities, Victor
Stott himself, who might have given me every
particular in accurate detail, had it not been for
those peculiarities of his which will be explained
fully in the proper place.

PART II

THE CHILDHOOD
OF THE WONDER

CHAPTER IV

I

STOKE-UNDERHILL lies in the flat of the valley that separates the Hampden from the Quainton Hills. The main road from London to Ailesworth does not pass through Stoke, but from the highway you can see the ascent of the bridge over the railway, down the vista of the straight mile of side road ; and, beyond, a glimpse of scattered cottages. That is all, and as a matter of fact, no one who is not keeping a sharp look-out would ever notice the village, for the eye is drawn to admire the bluff of Deane Hill, the highest point of the Hampdens, which lowers over the little hamlet of Stoke and gives it a second name ; and to the church tower of Chilborough Beacon, away to the right, another landmark.

The attraction which Stoke-Underhill held for Stott, lay not in its seclusion or its picturesqueness

65

but in its nearness to the County Ground. Stott could ride the two flat miles which separated him from the scene of his work in ten minutes, and Ailesworth station is only a mile beyond. So when he found that there was a suitable cottage to let in Stoke, he looked no farther for a home ; he was completely satisfied.

Stott's absorption in any matter that was occupying his mind, made him exceedingly careless about the detail of his affairs. He took the first cottage that offered when he looked for a home, he took the first woman who offered when he looked for a wife.

Stott was not an attractive man to women. He was short and plain, and he had an appearance of being slightly deformed, a " monkeyish " look, due to his build and his long arms. Still, he was famous, and might, doubtless, have been accepted by a dozen comely young women for that reason, even after his accident. But if Stott was unattractive to women, women were even more unattractive to Stott. " No opinion of women ? " he used to say. " Ever seen a gel try to throw a cricket ball ? You 'ave ? Well, ain't that enough to put you off women ? " That was Stott's intellectual standard ; physically, he had never felt drawn to women.

Ellen Mary Jakes exhibited no superiority over her sisters in the matter of throwing a cricket ball.

She was a friend of Ginger's mother, and she was a
woman of forty-two, who had long since been
relegated to some remote shelf of the matrimonial
exchange. But her physical disadvantages were out-
balanced by her mental qualities. Ellen Mary was
not a book-worm, she read nothing but the evening
and Sunday papers, but she had a reasoning and
intelligent mind.

She had often contemplated the state of matri-
mony, and had made more than one tentative essay
in that direction. She had walked out with three
or four sprigs of the Ailesworth bourgeoisie in her
time, and the shadow of middle-age had crept upon
her before she realised that however pliant her
disposition, her lack of physical charm put her at
the mercy of the first bright-eyed rival. At thirty-
five Ellen had decided, with admirable philosophy,
that marriage was not for her, and had assumed,
with apparent complacency, the outward evidences
of a dignified spinsterhood. She had discarded gay
hats and ribbons, imitation jewellery, unreliable
cheap shoes, and chill diaphanous stockings, and
had found some solace for her singleness in more
comfortable and suitable apparel.

When Ellen, a declared spinster of seven years'
standing, was first taken into the confidence of
Ginger Stott's mother, the scheme which she afterwards elaborated immediately presented itself to

her mind. This fact is a curious instance of Ellen Mary's mobility of intellect, and the student of heredity may here find matter for careful thought.*

The confidence in question was Ginger's declared intention of becoming the father of the world's greatest bowler. Mrs. Stott was a dark, garrulous, rather deaf little woman, with a keen eye for the main chance ; she might have become a successful woman of business if she had not been by nature both stingy and a cheat. When her son presented his determination, her first thought was to find some woman who would not dissipate her son's substance, and in her opinion—not expressed to Ginger—the advertised purpose of the contemplated marriage evidenced a wasteful disposition.

Mrs. Stott did not think of Ellen Mary as a possible daughter-in-law, but she did hold forth for an hour and three-quarters on the contemptible qualities of the young maidens, first of Ailesworth, and then with a wider swoop that was not justified by her

* A study of genius shows that in a percentage of cases so large as to exclude the possibility of coincidence, the exceptional man, whether in the world of action, of art, or of letters, seems to inherit his magnificent powers through the female line. Mr. Galton, it is true, did not make a great point of this curious observation, but the tendency of more recent analyses is all in the direction of confirming the hypothesis ; and it would seem to hold good in the converse proposition, namely, that the exceptional woman inherits her qualities from her father.

limited experience, of the girls of England, Scotland, and Ireland at large.

It required the flexible reasoning powers of Ellen Mary to find a solution of the problem. Any ordinary, average woman of forty-two, a declared spinster of seven years' standing, who had lived all her life in a provincial town, would have been mentally unable to realise the possibilities of the situation. Such a representative of the decaying sexual instinct would have needed the stimulus of courtship, at the least of some hint of preference displayed by the suitor. Ruled by the conventions which hold her sex in bondage, she would have deemed it unwomanly to make advances by any means other than innuendo, the subtle suggestions which are the instruments of her sex, but which are often too delicate to pierce the understanding of the obtuse and slow-witted male.

Ellen Mary stood outside the ruck that determines the destinies of all such typical representatives. She considered the idea presented to her by Mrs. Stott with an open and mobile intelligence. She weighed the character of Ginger, the possibilities of rejection, and the influence of Mrs. Stott ; and she gave no thought to the conventions, nor to the criticisms of Ailesworth society. When she had decided that such chances as she could calculate were in her favour, Ellen made up her mind, walked out to the County Ground one windy October forenoon, and discovered Ginger experimenting with grass seed in a shed off the pavilion.

In this shed she offered herself, while Ginger worked on, attentive but unresponsive. Perhaps she did not make an offer so much as state a case. A masterly case, without question ; for who can doubt that Stott, however procrastinating and unwilling to make a definite overture, must already have had some type of womanhood in his mind ; some conception, the seed of an ideal.

I find a quality of romance in this courageous and unusual wooing of Ellen Mary's ; but more, I find evidences of the remarkable quality of her intelligence. In other circumstances the name of Ellen Mary Jakes might have stood for individual achievement, instead, she is remembered as a common woman who *happened* to be the mother of Victor Stott. But when the facts are examined, can we say that chance entered ? If ever the birth of a child was deliberately designed by both parents, it was in the case under consideration. And what a strange setting to the inception.

Ellen Mary, a gaunt, tall, somewhat untidy woman, stood at the narrow door of the little shed off the Ailesworth pavilion ; with one hand, shoulder-high, she steadied herself against the door frame, with the other she continually pushed forward the rusty bonnet which had been loosened during her walk by the equinoctial gale that now tore at the door of the shed, and necessitated the employment of a wary foot to keep the door from slamming. With all these distractions she still made good her case, though she had to raise her voice above the multitudinous sounds of the wind, and though she had to address the unresponsive shoulders of a man who bent over shallow trays of earth set on a trestle table under the small and dirty window. It is heroic, but she had her reward in full measure. Presently her voice ceased, and she waited in silence for the answer that should decide her destiny. There was an interval broken only by the tireless passion of the wind, and then Ginger Stott, the best-known man in England, looked up and stared through the incrusted pane of glass before him at the dim vision of grass and swaying hedge. Unconsciously his hands strayed to his pockets, and then he said in a low, thoughtful voice : " Well ! I dunno why not."

II

Dr. O'Connell's face was white and drawn, and the redness of his eyelids more pronounced than ever as he faced Stott in the pale October dawn. He clutched at his beard with a nervous, combing movement, as he shook his head decidedly in answer to the question put to him.

" If it's not dead, now, 'twill be in very few hours," he said.

Stott was shaken by the feeble passion of a man who has spent many weary hours of suspense. His anger thrilled out in a feeble stream of hackneyed profanities.

O'Connell looked down on him with contempt. At sunrise, after a sleepless night, a man is a creature of unrealised emotions.

" Damn it, control yourself, man ! " growled O'Connell, himself uncontrolled, " your wife'll pull through with care, though she'll never have another child." O'Connell did not understand ; he was an Irishman, and no cricketer ; he had been called in because he had a reputation for his skill in obstetrics.

Stott stared at him fiercely. The two men seemed as if about to grapple desperately for life in the windy, grey twilight.

O'Connell recovered his self-control first, and began again to claw nervously at his beard. " Don't be a fool," he said, " it's only what you could expect. Her first child, and her a woman of near fifty." He returned to the upstairs room ; Stott seized his cap and went out into the chill world of sunrise.

" She'll do, if there are no complications," said O'Connell to the nurse, as he bent over the still, exhausted figure of Mrs. Stott. "She's a wonderful woman to have delivered such a child alive."

The nurse shivered, and avoiding any glance at the huddle that lay on an improvised sofa-bed, she said : " It can't live, can it ? "

O'Connell, still intent on his first patient, shook his head. "Never cried after delivery," he muttered "—the worst sign." He was silent for a moment and then he added : " But, to be sure, it's a freak of some kind." His scientific curiosity led him to make a further investigation. He left the bed and began to examine the huddle on the sofa-couch. Victor Stott owed his life, in the first instance, to this scientific curiosity of O'Connell's.

The nurse, a capable, but sentimental woman, turned to the window and looked out at the watery trickle of feeble sunlight that now illumined the wilderness of Stott's garden.

"Nurse !" The imperative call startled her ; she turned nervously.

" Yes, doctor ? " she said, making no movement towards him.

"Come here !" O'Connell was kneeling by the sofa. " There seems to be complete paralysis of all the motor centres," he went on; " but the child's not dead. We'll try artificial respiration."

The nurse overcame her repugnance by a visible effort. " Is it . . . is it worth while ? " she asked, regarding the flaccid, tumbled, wax-like thing, with its bloated, white globe of a skull. Every muscle of it was relaxed and limp, its eyes shut, its tiny jaw hanging. " Wouldn't it be better to let it die . . . ? "

O'Connell did not seem to hear her. He waved an impatient hand for her assistance. " Outside my experience," he muttered, " no heart-beat discernible, no breath . . . yet it is indubitably alive." He depressed the soft, plastic ribs and gave the feeble heart a gentle squeeze.

" It's beating," he ejaculated, after a pause, with an ear close to the little chest, " but still no breath ! Come ! "

The diminutive lungs were as readily open to suggestion as the wee heart : a few movements of the twigs they called arms, and the breath came. O'Connell closed the mouth and it remained closed, adjusted the limbs, and they stayed in the positions in which they were placed. At last he gently lifted the lids of the eyes.

The nurse shivered and drew back. Even O'Connell was startled, for the eyes that stared into his own seemed to be heavy with a brooding intelligence. . . .

Stott came back at ten o'clock, after a morose trudge through the misty rain. He found the nurse in the sitting-room.

" Doctor gone ? " he asked.

The nurse nodded.

" Dead, I suppose ? " Stott gave an upward twist of his head towards the room above.

The nurse shook her head.

" Can't live though ? " There was a note of faint hope in his voice.

The nurse drew herself together and sighed deeply. " Yes ! we believe it'll live, Mr. Stott," she said. " But . . . it's a very remarkable baby."

How that phrase always recurred !

III

There were no complications, but Mrs. Stott's recovery was not a rapid one. It was considered advisable that she should not see the child. She thought that they were lying to her, that the child was dead and, so, resigned herself. But her husband saw it.

He had never seen so young an infant before, and, just for one moment, he believed that it was a normal child.

" What an 'ead ! " was his first ejaculation, and then he realised the significance of that sign. Fear came into his eyes, and his mouth fell open. " 'Ere, I say, nurse, it's . . . it's a wrong 'un, ain't it ? " he gasped.

" I'm *sure* I can't tell you, Mr. Stott," broke out
the nurse hysterically. She had been feeding and
tending that curious baby for three hours, and she
was on the verge of a break-down. There was no
wet-nurse to be had, but a woman from the village
had been sent for. She was expected every moment.

" More like a tadpole than anything," mused the
unhappy father.

" Oh ! Mr. Stott, for goodness' sake, *don't*," cried
the nurse. " If you only knew. . . ."

" Knew what ? " questioned Stott, still staring
at the motionless figure of his son, who lay with
closed eyes, apparently unconscious.

" There's something—I don't know," began the
nurse, and then after a pause, during which she
seemed to struggle for some means of expression,
she continued with a sigh of utter weariness, " You'll
know when it opens its eyes. Oh ! Why doesn't
that woman come, the woman you sent for ? "

" She'll be 'ere directly," replied Stott. " What
d'you mean about there bein' something . . . something what ? "

" Uncanny," said the nurse without conviction.
" I do wish that woman would come. I've been up
the best part of the night, and now. . . ."

" Uncanny ? As how ? " persisted Stott.

" Not normal," explained the nurse. " I can't
tell you more than that."

" But 'ow ? What way ? "

He did not receive an answer then ; for the long
expected relief came at last, a great hulk of a woman,
who became voluble when she saw the child she had
come to nurse.

" Oh ! dear, oh ! dear," the stream began.
" How unforchnit, and 'er first, too. It'll be a idjit,
I'm afraid. Mrs. 'Arrison's third was the very spit
of it. . . ."

The stream ran on, but Stott heard no more. An
idiot ! He had fathered an idiot ! That was the
end of his dreams and ambitions ! He had had an
hour's sleep on the sitting-room sofa. He went out
to his work at the County Ground with a heart full
of blasphemy.

When he returned at four o'clock he met the stout
woman on the doorstep. She put up a hand to her
rolling breast, closed her eyes tightly, and gasped
as though completely overcome by this trifling
rencounter.

" 'Ow is it ? " questioned the obsessed Stott.

" Oh dear ! Oh dear ! " panted the stout woman,
" the leas' thing upsets me this afternoon. . . ."
She wandered away into irrelevant fluency, but
Stott was autocratic ; his insistent questions overcame the inertia of even Mrs. Reade at last. The
substance of her information, freed from extraneous
matter, was as follows :

" Oh ! 'ealthy ?   It'll live, I've no doubt, if that's
what you mean ; but 'elpless . . . !   There, 'elpless
is no word. . . . Learn 'im to take the bottle, learn
'im to close 'is 'ands, learn 'im to go to sleep, learn
'im everythink.   I've never seen nothink like it,
never in all my days, and I've 'elped to bring a few
into the world. . . . I can't begin to tell you about
it, Mr. Stott, and that's the solemn truth.   When
'e first looked at me, I near 'ad a faint.   A old-
fashioned, wise sort of look as 'e might 'a been a
'undred.   ' Lord 'elp us, nurse,' I says, ' Lord help
us.'   I was that opset, I didn't rightly know what
I was a-saying. . . ."

Stott pushed past the agitated Mrs. Reade, and
went into the sitting-room.   He had had neither
breakfast nor lunch ; there was no sign of any
preparation for his tea, and the fireplace was grey
with the cinders of last night's fire.   For some
minutes he sat in deep despondency, a hero faced
with the uncompromising detail of domestic neglect.
Then he rose and called to the nurse.

She appeared at the head of the steep, narrow
staircase.   " Sh ! " she warned, with a finger to
her lips.

" I'm goin' out again," said Stott in a slightly
modulated voice.

" Mrs. Reade's coming back presently," replied
the nurse, and looked over her shoulder.

" Want me to wait ? " asked Stott.

The nurse came down a few steps. " It's only in case any one was wanted," she began, " I've got two of 'em on my hands, you see. They're both doing well as far as that goes. Only . . . " She broke off and drifted into small talk. Ever and again she stopped and listened intently, and looked back towards the half-open door of the upstairs room.

Stott fidgeted, and then, as the flow of conversation gave no sign of running dry, he damned it abruptly. " Look 'ere, miss," he said, " I've 'ad nothing to eat since last night."

" Oh ! dear ! " ejaculated the nurse. " If—perhaps, if you'd just stay here and listen, I could get you something." She seemed relieved to have some excuse for coming down.

While she bustled about the kitchen, Stott, half-way upstairs, stayed and listened. The house was very silent, the only sound was the hushed clatter made by the nurse in the kitchen. There was an atmosphere of wariness about the place that affected even so callous a person as Stott. He listened with strained attention, his eyes fixed on the half-open door. He was not an imaginative man, but he was beset with apprehension as to what lay behind that door. He looked for something inhuman that might come crawling through the aperture, something

grotesque, preternaturally wise and threatening—
something horribly unnatural.

The window of the upstairs room was evidently
open, and now and again the door creaked faintly.
When that happened Stott gripped the handrail,
and grew damp and hot. He looked always at the
shadows under the door—if it crawled. . . .

The nurse stood at the door of the sitting-room
while Stott ate, and presently Mrs. Reade came
grunting and panting up the brick path.

" I'm going out, now," said Stott resolutely, and
he rose to his feet, though his meal was barely
finished.

" You'll be back before Mrs. Reade goes ? " asked
the nurse, and passed a hand over her tired eyes.
" She'll be here till ten o'clock. I'm going to lie
down."

" I'll be back by ten," Stott assured her as he
went out.

He did come back at ten o'clock, but he was
stupidly drunk.

IV

The Stotts' cottage was no place to live in during
the next few days, but the nurse made one stipulation ; Mr. Stott must come home to sleep. He slept
on an improvised bed in the sitting-room, and during
the night the nurse came down many times and

listened to the sound of his snores. She would put
her ear against the door, and rest her nerves with the
thought of human companionship. Sometimes she
opened the door quietly and watched him as he
slept. Except at night, when he was rarely quite
sober, Stott only visited his cottage once a day, at
lunch time ; from seven in the morning till ten at
night he remained in Ailesworth save for this one
call of inquiry.

It was such a still house. Ellen Mary only spoke
when speech was absolutely required, and then her
words were the fewest possible, and were spoken in
a whisper. The child made no sound of any kind.
Even Mrs. Reade tried to subdue her stertorous
breathing, to move with less ponderous quakings.
The neighbours told her she looked thinner.

Little wonder that during the long night vigil
the nurse, moving silently between the two upstairs
rooms, should pause on the landing and lean over
the handrail ; little wonder that she should give a
long sigh of relief when she heard the music of Stott's
snore ascend from the sitting-room.

O'Connell called twice every day during the first
week, not because it was necessary for him to visit
his two patients, but because the infant fascinated
him. He would wait for it to open its eyes, and then
would get up and leave the room hurriedly. Always
he intended to return the infant's stare, but when

6

the opportunity was given to him, he always rose
and left the room—no matter how long and deliberately he had braced himself to another course
of action.

It was on a Thursday that the baby was born, and
it was on the following Thursday that the circumstance of the household was reshaped.

O'Connell came in the morning, full of resolution.
After he had pronounced Mrs. Stott well on the way
to recovery, he paid the usual visit to his younger
patient. The child lay, relaxed, at full length, in
the little cot which had been provided for him. His
eyes were, as usual, closed, and he had all the appearance of the ordinary hydrocephalic idiot.

O'Connell sat down by the cot, listened to the
child's breathing and heart-beat, lifted and let fall
again the lax wrist, turned back the eyelid, revealing
only the white of the upturned eyeball, and then
composed himself to await the natural waking of
the child, if it were asleep—always a matter of un-
certainty.

The nurse stood near him, silent, but she looked
away from the cot.

"Hydrocephalus!" murmured O'Connell, staring
at his tiny patient, "hydrocephalus, without a
doubt. Eh? nurse!"

"Yes, perhaps! I don't know, doctor."

"Oh, not a doubt of it, not a doubt," repeated

O'Connell, and then came a flicker of the child's eyelids and a weak crumpling of the tiny hand.

O'Connell caught his breath and clawed at his beard; "Hydrocephalus," he muttered with set jaw and drawn eyebrows.

The tiny hand straightened with a movement that suggested the recovery of crushed grass, the mouth opened with a microscopic yawn, and then the eyelids were slowly raised and a steady unwavering stare of profoundest intelligence met O'Connell's gaze.

He clenched his hands, shifted in his chair, and then rose abruptly and turned to the window.

"I—it won't be necessary for me to come again, nurse," he said curtly; "they are both doing perfectly well."

"Not come again?" There was dismay in the nurse's question.

"No! No! It's unnecessary. . . ." He broke off, and made for the door without another glance in the direction of the cot.

Nurse followed him downstairs.

"If I'm wanted—you can easily send for me," said O'Connell, as he went out. As he moved away he dragged at his beard and murmured "Hydrocephalus, not a doubt of it."

Following his departure, Mrs. Reade heard curious and most unwonted laughter, and cautiously blundered downstairs to investigate. She found the nurse in an advanced condition of hysteria, laughing, gurgling, weeping, and intermittently crying in a shrill voice: " Oh ! Lord have mercy ; Lord ha' mercy ! "

" Now, see you 'ere, my dear," said Mrs. Reade, when nurse had been recovered to a red-eyed sanity, " it's time she was told. I've never 'eld with keepin' it from 'er, myself, and I've 'ad more experience than many. . . ." Mrs. Reade argued with abundant recourse to parenthesis.

" Is she strog edough ? " asked the nurse, still with tears in her voice ; " cad she bear the sight of hib ? " She blew her nose vigorously, and then continued with greater clearness : " I'm afraid it may turn her head."

Out of her deep store of wisdom, Mrs. Reade produced a fact which she elaborated and confirmed by apt illustration, adducing more particularly the instance of Mrs. Harrison's third. " She's 'is mother," was the essence of her argument, a fact of deep and strange significance.

The nurse yielded, and so the circumstance of Stott's household was changed, and Stott himself was once more able to come home to meals.

The nurse, wisely, left all diplomacy to the capable Mrs. Reade, a woman specially fitted by nature for the breaking of news. She delivered a long, a record-breaking circumlocution, and it seemed that Ellen Mary, who lay with closed eyes, gathered no hint of its import. But when the impressive harangue was slowly rustling to collapse like an exhausted balloon, she opened her eyes and said quite clearly,

" What's wrong with 'im, then ? "

The question had the effect of reinflation, but at last the child itself was brought, and it was open-eyed.

The supreme ambition of all great women—and have not all women the potentialities of greatness ?—is to give birth to a god. That ambition it is which is marred by the disappointing birth of a female child—when the man-child is born, there is always hope, and slow is the realisation of failure. That realisation never came to Ellen Mary. She accepted her child with the fear that is adoration. When she dropped her eyes before her god's search-ing glance, she did it in reverence. She hid her faith from the world, but in her heart she believed that she was blessed above all women. In secret, she worshipped the inscrutable wonder that had used her as the instrument of his incarnation. Per-haps she was right. . . .

CHAPTER V

I

THE village of Stoke was no whit intimidated by the news that Mrs. Reade sowed abroad. The women exclaimed and chattered, the men gaped and shook their heads, the children hung about the ruinous gate that shut them out from the twenty-yard strip of garden which led up to Stott's cottage. Curiosity was the dominant emotion. Any excuse was good enough to make friendly overtures, but the babe remained invisible to all save Mrs. Reade ; and the village community kept open ears while the lust of its eyes remained, perforce, unsatisfied. If Stott's gate slammed in the wind, every door that commanded a view of that gate was opened, and heads appeared, and bare arms—the indications of women who nodded to each other, shook their heads, pursed their lips and withdrew for the time to attend the pressure of household duty. Later, even that gate slamming would reinvigorate the gossip of backyards and front doorways.

The first stranger to force an entry was the rector. He was an Oxford man who, in his youth, had been an ardent disciple of the school that attempts the reconciliation of Religion and Science. He had been ambitious, but nature had predetermined his career by giving him a head of the wrong shape. At Oxford his limitations had not been clearly defined, and on the strength of a certain speech at the Union, he crept into a London west-end curacy. There he attempted to demonstrate the principle of reconciliation from the pulpit, but his vicar and his bishop soon recognised that excellent as were his intentions, he was doing better service to agnosticism than to his own religion. In consequence he was vilely marooned on the savage island of Stoke-Underhill, where he might preach as much science as he would to the natives, for there was no fear of their comprehending him. Fifteen years of Stoke had brought about a reaction. Nature had made him a feeble fanatic, and he was now as ardent an opponent of science as he had once been a defender. In his little mind he believed that his early reading had enabled him to understand all the weaknesses of the scientific position. His name was Percy Crashaw.

Mrs. Stott could not deny her rector the right of entry, and he insisted on seeing the infant, who was not yet baptised—a shameful neglect, according to Crashaw, for the child was nearly six weeks old. Nor had Mrs. Stott been "churched." Crashaw had good excuse for pressing his call.

Mrs. Stott refused to face the village. She knew that the place was all agape, eager to stare at what they considered some "new kind of idiot." Let them wait, was Ellen Mary's attitude. Her pride was a later development. In those early weeks she feared criticism.

But she granted Crashaw's request to see the child, and after the interview (the term is precise) the rector gave way on the question of a private ceremony, though he had indignantly opposed the scheme when it was first mooted. It may be that he conceived an image of himself with that child in his arms, the cynosure of a packed congregation. . .

Crashaw was one of the influences that hastened the Stotts' departure from Stoke. He was so indiscreet. After the christening he would talk. His attitude is quite comprehensible. He, the lawgiver of Stoke, had been thwarted. He had to find apology for the private baptism he had denied to many a sickly infant. Moreover, the Stotts had broken another of his ordinances, for father and mother had stood as god-parents to their own child, and Crashaw himself had been the second god-father ordained as necessary by the rubric. He had given way on these important points so weakly ; he had to find excuse, and he talked himself into a false belief with regard to the child he had baptised.

He began with his wife. " I would allow more latitude to medical men," he said. " In such a case as this child of the Stotts, for instance ; it becomes a burden on the community, I might say a danger, yes, a positive danger. I am not sure whether I was right in administering the holy sacrament of baptism. . . ."

" Oh ! Percy ! Surely . . . " began Mrs. Crashaw.

" One moment, my dear," protested the rector, " I have not fully explained the circumstances of the case." And as he warmed to his theme the image of Victor Stott grew to a fearful grotesqueness. It loomed as a threat over the community and the church. Crashaw quoted, inaccurately, statistics of the growth of lunacy, and then went off at a tangent into the theory of possession by evil spirits. Since his rejection of science, he had lapsed into certain forms of mediævalism, and he now began to dally with a theory of a malign incarnation which he elaborated until it became an article of his faith.

To his poorer parishioners he spoke in vague terms, but he changed their attitude ; he filled them with overawed terror. They were intensely curious still, but, now, when the gate was slammed, one saw a face pressed to the window, the door remained fast ; and the children no longer clustered round that gate, but dared each other to run past it ; which they did, the girls with a scream, the boys with a jeering " Yah—ah ! " a boast of intrepidity.

This change of temper was soon understood by the persons most concerned. Stott grumbled and grew more morose. He had never been intimate with the villagers, and now he avoided any intercourse with them. His wife kept herself aloof, and her child sheltered from profane observation. Naturally, this attitude of the Stotts fostered suspicion. Even the hardiest sceptic in the taproom of the Challis Arms began to shake his head, to concede that there " moight be soomething in it."

Yet the departure from Stoke might have been postponed indefinitely, if it had not been for another intrusion. Both Stott and his wife were ready to take up a new idea, but they were slow to conceive it.

II

The intruder was the local magnate, the landlord of Stoke, Wenderby, Chilborough, a greater part of Ailesworth, two or three minor parishes, and, incidentally, of Pym.

This magnate, Henry Challis, was a man of some

scholarship, whose ambition had been smothered by the heaviness of his possessions. He had a remarkably fine library at Challis Court, but he made little use of it, for he spent the greater part of his time in travel. In appearance he was rather an ungainly man; his great head and the bulk of his big shoulders were something too heavy for his legs.

Crashaw regarded his patron with mixed feelings. For Challis, the man of property, the man of high connections, of intimate associations with the world of science and letters, Crashaw had a feeling of awed respect; but in private he inveighed against the wickedness of Challis, the agnostic, the decadent.

When Victor Stott was nearly three months old, the rector met his patron one day on the road between Chilborough and Stoke. It was three years since their last meeting, and Crashaw noticed that in the interval Challis's pointed beard had become streaked with grey.

" Hallo! How d'ye do, Crashaw?" was the squire's casual greeting. "How is the Stoke microcosm?"

Crashaw smiled subserviently; he was never quite at his ease in Challis's presence. " Rari nantes in gurgite vasto," was the tag he found in answer to the question put. However great his contempt for Challis's way of life, in his presence Crashaw was often oppressed with a feeling of inferiority, a feeling which he fought against but could not subdue. The Latin tag was an attempt to win appreciation, it represented a boast of equality.

Challis correctly evaluated the rector's attitude; it was with something of pity in his mind that he turned and walked beside him.

There was but one item of news from Stoke, and it soon came to the surface. Crashaw phrased his description of Victor Stott in terms other than those he used in speaking to his wife or to his parishioners; but the undercurrent of his virulent superstition did not escape Challis, and the attitude of the villagers was made perfectly plain.

"Hm!" was Challis's comment, when the flow of words ceased, "nigroque simillima cygno, eh?"

"Ah! of course, you sneer at our petty affairs," said Crashaw.

"By no means. I should like to see this black swan of Stoke," replied Challis. "Anything so exceptional interests me."

"No doubt Mrs. Stott would be proud to exhibit the horror," said Crashaw. He had a gleam of satisfaction in the thought that even the great Henry Challis might be scared. That would, indeed, be a triumph.

"If Mrs. Stott has no objection, of course," said Challis. "Shall we go there, now?"

III

The visit of Henry Challis marked the first advent of Ellen Mary's pride in the exhibition of her wonder. After the King and the Royal Family—superhuman beings, infinitely remote—the great landlord of the neighbourhood stood as a symbol of temporal power to the whole district. The budding socialist of the taproom might sneer, and make threat that the time was coming when he, the boaster, and Challis, the landlord, would have equal rights ; but in public the socialist kow-towed to his master with a submission no less obsequious than that of the humblest conservative on the estate.

Mrs. Stott dropped a deep curtsy when, opening the door to the autocratic summons of Crashaw's rat-a-tat, she saw the great man of the district at her threshold. Challis raised his hat. Crashaw did not imitate his example ; he was all officiousness, he had the air of a chief superintendent of police.

" Oh ! Mrs. Stott, we should like to come in for a few minutes. Mr. Challis would like to see your child."

" Damn the fool ! " was Challis's thought, but he gave it less abrupt expression. " That is, of course, if it is quite convenient to you, Mrs. Stott. I can come at some other time . . . ."

" Please walk in, sir," replied Mrs. Stott, and curtsied again as she stood aside.

Superintendent Crashaw led the way . . . .

Challis called again next day, by himself this time ; and the day after he dropped in at six o'clock while Mr. and Mrs. Stott were at tea. He put them at their ease by some magic of his personality, and insisted that they should continue their meal while he sat among the collapsed springs of the horsehair armchair. He leaned forward and swung his stick between his knees as it were a pendulum, and shot out questions as to the Stotts' relations with the neighbours. And always he had an attentive eye on the cradle that stood near the fire.

" The neighbours are not highly intelligent, I suspect," said Challis. " Even Mr. Crashaw, I fancy, does not appreciate the—peculiarities of the situation."

" He's worse than any," interpolated Stott. Ellen Mary sat in shadow ; there was a new light in her eyes, a foretaste of glory.

" Ah ! a little narrow, a little dogmatic, no doubt," replied Challis. " I was going to propose that you might prefer to live at Pym."

" Much farther for me," muttered Stott. He had mixed with nobility on the cricket field, and was not overawed.

" No doubt ; but you have other interests to con-

sider, interests of far greater importance." Challis
shifted his gaze from the cradle, and looked Stott in
the face. " I understand that Mrs. Stott does not
care to take her child out in the village. Isn't that
so ? "

" Yes, sir," replied Ellen, to whom this question
was addressed. " I don't care to make an exhibition
of 'im."

" Quite right, quite right," went on Challis, " but
it is very necessary that the child should have air.
I consider it very necessary, a matter of the first
importance that the child should have air," he
repeated. His gaze had shifted back to the cradle
again. The child lay with open eyes, staring up at
the ceiling.

" Now, there is an excellent cottage at Pym which
I will have put in repair for you at once," continued
Challis. " It is one of two together, but next door
there are only old Metcalfe and his wife and daughter,
who will give you no trouble. And really, Mrs.
Stott," he tore his regard from the cradle for a
moment, " there is no reason in the world why you
should fear the attention of your neighbours. Here,
in Stoke, I admit, they have been under a complete
misapprehension, but I fancy that there were special
reasons for that. In Pym you will have few neighbours, and you need not, I'm sure, fear their criticism."

"They got one idiot there, already," Stott remarked somewhat sulkily.

"You surely do not regard your own child as likely to develop into an idiot, Stott!" Challis's tone was one of rebuke.

Stott shifted in his chair and his eyes flickered uncertainly in the direction of the cradle. "Dr. O'Connell says 'twill," he said.

"When did he see the child last?" asked Challis.

"Not since 'twere a week old, sir," replied Ellen.

"In that case his authority goes for nothing, and, then, by the way, I suppose the child has not been vaccinated?"

"Not yet, sir."

"Better have that done. Get Walters. I'll make myself responsible. I'll get him to come."

Before Challis left, it was decided that the Stotts should move to Pym in February.

When the great landowner had gone, Mrs. Stott looked wistfully at her husband.

"You ain't fair to the child, George," she said. "There's more than you or any one sees, more than Mr. Challis, even."

Stott stared moodily into the fire.

"And it won't be so out of the way far for you, at Pym, with your bike," she continued; "and we *can't* stop 'ere."

" We might 'a took a place in Ailesworth," said
Stott.

" But it'll be so much 'ealthier for 'im up at Pym,"
protested Ellen. " It'll be fine air up there for
'im."

" Oh! 'im. Yes, all right for '*im*," said Stott,
and spat into the fire. Then he took his cap and
went out. He kept his eyes away from the cradle.

IV

Harvey Walters lived in Wenderby, but his con-
sulting-rooms were in Harley Street, and he did not
practise in his own neighbourhood ; nevertheless he
vaccinated Victor Stott to oblige Challis.

" Well ? " asked Challis a few days later, " what
do you make of him, Walters ? No clichés, now,
and no professional jargon."

" Candidly, I don't know," replied Walters, after
a thoughtful interval.

" How many times have you seen him ? "

" Four, altogether."

" Good patient ? Healthy flesh and that sort of
thing ? "

" Splendid."

" Did he look you in the eyes ? "

" Once, only once, the first time I visited the
house."

7

Challis nodded. " My own experience, exactly. And did you return that look of his ? "

" Not willingly. It was, I confess, not altogether a pleasant experience."

" Ah ! "

Challis was silent for a few moments, and it was Walters who took up the interrogatory.

" Challis ! "

" Yes ? "

" Have you, now, some feeling of, shall I say, distaste for the child ? Do you feel that you have no wish to see it again ? "

" Is it that exactly ? " parried Challis.

" If not, what is it ? " asked Walters.

" In my own case," said Challis, " I can find an analogy only in my attitude towards my ' head ' at school. In his presence I was always intimidated by my consciousness of his superior learning. I felt unpleasantly ignorant, small, negligible. Curiously enough, I see something of the same expression of feeling in the attitude of that feeble Crashaw to myself. Well, one makes an attempt at self-assertion, a kind of futile bragging ; and one knows the futility of it—at the time. But, afterwards, one finds excuse and seeks to belittle the personality and attainment of the person one feared. At school we did not love the ' head,' and, as schoolboys will, we were always trying to run him down. ' Next time he rags me, I'll cheek him,' was our usual boast—but we never did.   Let's be honest, Walters, are not you and I exhibiting much the same attitude towards this extraordinary child ?   Didn't he pro-duce the effect upon you that I've described ? Didn't you have a little of the ' fifth form ' feeling, —a boy under examination ? "

Walters smiled and screwed his mouth on one side. " The thing is so absurd," he said.

" That is what we used to say at school," replied Challis.

v

The Stotts' move to Pym was not marked by any incident.   Mrs. Stott and her boy were not unduly stared upon as they left Stoke—the children were in school—and their entry into the new cottage was uneventful.

They moved on a Thursday.   On Sunday morning they had their first visitor.

He came mooning round the fence that guarded the Stotts' garden from the little lane—it was hardly more than a footpath.   He had a great shapeless head that waggled heavily on his shoulders, his eyes were lustreless, and his mouth hung open, frequently his tongue lagged out.   He made strange, inhuman noises.   " A-ba-ba," was his nearest approach to speech.

" Now, George," called Mrs. Stott, " look at that. It's Mrs. 'Arrison's boy what Mrs. Reade's spoke about. Now, is 'e anythink like . . . " she paused, " anythink like 'im ? " and she indicated the cradle in the sitting-room.

" What's 'e want, 'angin' round 'ere ? " replied Stott, disregarding the comparison. " 'Ere, get off," he called, and he went into the garden and picked up a stick.

The idiot shambled away.

CHAPTER VI

HIS FATHER'S DESERTION

I

THE strongest of all habits is that of acquiescence. It is this habit of submission which explains the admired patience and long-suffering of the abjectly poor. The lower the individual falls, the more unconquerable becomes the inertia of mind which interferes between him and revolt against his condition. All the miseries of the flesh, even starvation, seem preferable to the making of an effort great enough to break this habit of submission.

Ginger Stott was not poor. For a man in his station of life he was unusually well provided for, but in him the habit of acquiescence was strongly rooted. Before his son was a year old, Stott had grown to loathe his home, to dread his return to it, yet it did not occur to him until another year had passed that he could, if he would, set up another establishment on his own account ; that he could, for instance, take a room in Ailesworth, and leave his wife and child in the cottage. For two years he did not begin to think of this idea, and then it was suddenly forced upon him.

Ever since they had overheard those strangely intelligent self-communings, the Stotts had been perfectly aware that their wonderful child could talk if he would. Ellen Mary, pondering that single expression, had read a world of meaning into her son's murmurs of " learning." In her simple mind she understood that his deliberate withholding of speech was a reserve against some strange manifestation.

The manifestation, when it came, was as remarkable as it was unexpected.

The arm-chair in which Henry Challis had once sat was a valued possession, dedicated by custom to the sole use of George Stott. Ever since he had been married, Stott had enjoyed the full and undisputed use of that chair. Except at his meals, he never sat in any other, and he had formed a fixed habit of throwing himself into that chair immediately on his return from his work at the County Ground.

One evening in November, however, when his son was just over two years old, Stott found his sacred chair occupied. He hesitated a moment, and then went in to the kitchen to find his wife.

" That child's in my chair," he said.

Ellen was setting the tray for her husband's
tea. " Yes . . . I know," she replied. " I—I did
mention it, but 'e 'asn't moved."

" Well, take 'im out," ordered Stott, but he
dropped his voice.

" Does it matter ? " asked his wife. " Tea's just
ready. Time that's done 'e'll be ready for 'is
bath."

" Why can't you move 'im ? " persisted Stott
gloomily. " 'E knows it's my chair."

" There ! kettle's boilin', come in and 'ave your
tea," equivocated the diplomatic Ellen.

During the progress of the meal, the child still sat
quietly in his father's chair, his little hands resting
on his knees, his eyes wide open, their gaze abstracted,
as usual, from all earthly concerns.

But after tea Stott was heroic. He had reached
the limit of his endurance. One of his deep-seated
habits was being broken, and with it snapped his
habit of acquiescence. He rose to his feet and faced
his son with determination, and Stott had a bull-dog
quality about him that was not easily defeated.

" Look 'ere ! Get out ! " he said. " That's *my*
chair ! "

The child very deliberately withdrew his attention
from infinity and regarded the dogged face and set
jaw of his father. Stott returned the stare for the

fraction of a second, and then his eyes wavered and dropped, but he maintained his resolution.

" You got to get out," he said, " or I'll lift you."

Ellen Mary gripped the edge of the table, but she made no attempt to interfere.

There was a tense, strained silence. Then Stott began to breathe heavily. He lifted his long arms for a moment and raised his eyes, he even made a tentative step towards the usurped chair.

The child sat calm, motionless; his eyes were fixed upon his father's face with a sublime, unalterable confidence.

Stott's arms fell to his sides again, he shuffled his feet. One more effort he made, a sudden, vicious jerk, as though he would do the thing quickly and be finished with it; then he shivered, his resolution broke, and he shambled evasively to the door.

" God damn," he muttered. At the door he turned for an instant, swore again in the same words, and went out into the night.

To Stott, moodily pacing the Common, this thing was incomprehensible, some horrible infraction of the law of normal life, something to be condemned; altered, if possible. It was unprecedented, and it was, therefore, wrong, unnatural, diabolic, a violation of the sound principles which uphold human society.

To Ellen Mary it was merely a miracle, the fore-shadowing of greater miracles to come. And to her was manifested, also, a minor miracle, for when his father had gone, the child looked at his mother and gave out his first recorded utterance.

" 'Oo *is* God ? " he said.

Ellen Mary tried to explain, but before she had stammered out many words, her son abstracted his gaze, climbed down out of the chair, and intimated with his usual grunt that he desired his bath and his bed.

II

The depths of Stott were stirred that night. He had often said that " he wouldn't stand it much longer," but the words were a mere formula : he had never even weighed their intention. As he paced the Common, he muttered them again to the night, with new meaning; he saw new possi-bilities, and saw that they were practicable. " I've 'ad enough," was his new phrase, and he added another that evidenced his new attitude. " Why not ? " he said again and again. " And why not ? "

Stott's mind was not analytical. He did not examine his problem, weigh this and that and draw a balanced deduction. He merely saw a picture of peace and quiet, in a room at Ailesworth, in convenient proximity to his work (he made an admirable groundsman and umpire, his work absorbed him) and, perhaps, he conceived some dim ideal of pleasant evenings spent in the companionship of those who thought in the same terms as himself ; whose speech was of form, averages, the preparation of wickets, and all the detail of cricket ; who shared in his one interest.

Stott's ambition to have a son and to teach him the mysteries of his father's success had been dwindling for some time past. On this night it was finally put aside. Stott's " I've 'ad enough " may be taken to include that frustrated ideal. No more experiments for him, was the pronouncement that summed up his decision.

Still there were difficulties. Economically he was free, he could allow his wife thirty shillings a week, more than enough for her support and that of her child ; but—what would she say, how would she take his determination ? A determination it was, not a proposal. And the neighbours, what would they say ? Stott anticipated a fuss. " She'll say I've married 'er, and it's my duty to stay by 'er," was his anticipation of his wife's attitude. He did not profess to understand the ways of the sex, but some rumours of misunderstandings between husbands and wives of his own class had filtered through his absorption in cricket.

He stumbled home with a mind prepared for dissension.

He found his wife stitching by the fire. The door at the foot of the stairs was closed. The room presented an aspect of cleanly, cheerful comfort ; but Stott entered with dread, not because he feared to meet his wife, but because there was a terror sleeping in that house.

His armchair was empty now, but he hesitated before he sat down in it. He took off his cap and rubbed the seat and back of the chair vigorously : a child of evil had polluted it, the chair might still hold enchantment. . . .

" 'I've 'ad enough," was his preface, and there was no need for any further explanation.

Ellen Mary let her hands fall into her lap, and stared dreamily at the fire.

" I'm sorry it's come to this, George," she said, " but it 'asn't been my fault no more'n it's been your'n. Of course I've seen it a-comin', and I knowed it '*ad* to be, some time ; but I don't think there need be any 'ard words over it. I don't expec' you to understand 'im, no more'n I do myself—it isn't in nature as you should, but all said and done, there's no bones broke, and if we 'ave to part, there's no reason as we shouldn't part peaceable."

That speech said nearly everything. Afterwards

it was only a question of making arrangements, and in that there was no difficulty.

Another man might have felt a little hurt, a little neglected by the absence of any show of feeling on his wife's part, but Stott passed it by. He was singularly free from all sentimentality; certain primitive, human emotions seem to have played no part in his character. At this moment he certainly had no thought that he was being carelessly treated; he wanted to be free from the oppression of that horror upstairs—so he figured it—and the way was made easy for him.

He nodded approval, and made no sign of any feeling.

"I shall go to-morrer," he said, and then, "I'll sleep down 'ere to-night." He indicated the sofa upon which he had slept for so many nights at Stoke, after his tragedy had been born to him.

Ellen Mary had said nearly everything, but when she had made up a bed for her husband in the sitting-room, she paused, candle in hand, before she bade him good-night.

"Don't wish 'im 'arm, George," she said. "'E's different from us, and we don't understand 'im proper, but some day——"

"I don't wish 'im no 'arm," replied Stott, and shuddered. "I don't wish 'im no 'arm," he re-

peated, as he kicked off the boot he had been
unlacing.

"You mayn't never see 'im again," added Ellen
Mary.

Stott stood upright. In his socks, he looked
noticeably shorter than his wife. "I suppose not,"
he said, and gave a deep sigh of relief. "Well,
thank Gawd for that, anyway."

Ellen Mary drew her lips together. For some dim,
unrealised reason, she wished her husband to leave
the cottage with a feeling of goodwill towards the
child, but she saw that her wish was little likely to
be fulfilled.

"Well, good-night, George," she said, after a few
seconds of silence, and she added pathetically, as
she turned at the foot of the stairs : "Don't wish
'im no harm."

"I won't," was all the assurance she received.

When she had gone, and the door was closed
behind her, Stott padded silently to the window and
looked out. A young moon was dipping into a bank
of cloud, and against the feeble brightness he could
see an uncertain outline of bare trees. He pulled
the curtain across the window, and turned back to
the warm cheerfulness of the room.

"Shan't never see 'im again," he murmured,
"thank Gawd !" He undressed quietly, blew out
the lamp and got between the sheets of his improvised

bed. For some minutes he stared at the leaping shadows on the ceiling. He was wondering why he had ever been afraid of the child. "After all, 'e's only a blarsted freak," was the last thought in his mind before he fell asleep.

With that pronouncement Stott passes out of the history of the Hampdenshire Wonder. He was in many ways an exceptional man, and his name will always be associated with the splendid successes of Hampdenshire cricket, both before and after the accident that destroyed his career as a bowler. He was not spoiled by his triumphs: those two years of celebrity never made Stott conceited, and there are undoubtedly many traits in his character which call for our admiration. He is still in his prime, an active agent in finding talent for his county, and in developing that talent when found. Hampdenshire has never come into the field with weak bowling, and all the credit belongs to Ginger Stott.

One sees that he was not able to appreciate the wonderful gifts of his own son, but Stott was an ignorant man, and men of intellectual attainment failed even as Stott failed in this respect. Ginger Stott was a success in his own walk of life, and that fact should command our admiration. It is not for us to judge whether his attainments were more or less noble than the attainments of his son.

III

One morning, two days after Stott had left the cottage, Ellen Mary was startled by the sudden entrance of her child into the sitting-room. He toddled in hastily from the garden, and pointed with excitement through the window.

Ellen Mary was frightened ; she had never seen her child other than deliberate, calm, judicial, in all his movements. In a sudden spasm of motherly love she bent to pick him up, to caress him.

" No," said the Wonder, with something that approached disgust in his tone and attitude. " No," he repeated. " What's 'e want 'angin' round 'ere ? Send 'im off." He pointed again to the window.

Ellen Mary looked out and saw a grinning, slobbering obscenity at the gate. Stott had scared the idiot away, but in some curious, inexplicable manner he had learned that his persecutor and enemy had gone, and he had returned, and had made overtures to the child that walked so sedately up and down the path of the little garden.

Ellen Mary went out. " You be off," she said.

" A-ba, a-ba-ba," bleated the idiot, and pointed at the house.

" Be off, I tell you ! " said Ellen Mary fiercely. But still the idiot babbled and pointed.

Ellen Mary stooped to pick up a stick. The idiot blenched; he understood that movement well enough, though it was a stone he anticipated, not a stick ; with a foolish cry he dropped his arms and slouched away down the lane.

CHAPTER VII

HIS DEBT TO HENRY CHALLIS

I

CHALLIS was out of England for more than three years after that one brief intrusion of his into the affairs of Mr. and Mrs. Stott. During the interval he was engaged upon those investigations, the results of which are embodied in his monograph on the primitive peoples of the Melanesian Archipelago. It may be remembered that he followed Dr. W. H. R. Rivers' and Dr. C. G. Seligmann's inquiry into the practice and theory of native customs. Challis developed his study more particularly with reference to the earlier evolution of Totemism, and he was able by his patient work among the Polynesians of Tikopia and Ontong Java, and his comparisons of those sporadic tribes with the Papuasians of Eastern New Guinea, to correct some of the inferences with regard to the origins of exogamy made by Dr. J. G. Frazer in his great work on that subject, published

8

some years before. A summary of Challis's argument may be found in vol. li. of the *Journal of the Royal Anthropological Institute.*

When he returned to England, Challis shut himself up at Chilborough. He had engaged a young Cambridge man, Gregory Lewes, as his secretary and librarian, and the two devoted all their time to planning, writing, and preparing the monograph referred to.

In such circumstances it is hardly remarkable that Challis should have completely forgotten the existence of the curious child which had intrigued his interest nearly four years earlier, and it was not until he had been back at Challis Court for more than eight months, that the incursion of Percy Crashaw revived his memory of the phenomenon.

The library at Challis Court occupies a suite of three rooms. The first and largest of the three is part of the original structure of the house. Its primitive use had been that of a chapel, a one-storey building jutting out from the west wing. This Challis had converted into a very practicable library with a continuous gallery running round at a height of seven feet from the floor, and in it he had succeeded in arranging some 20,000 volumes. But as his store of books grew—and at one period it had grown very rapidly—he had been forced to build, and so he had added first one and then the other of the two additional rooms which became necessary. Outside, the wing had the appearance of an unduly elongated chapel, as he had continued the original roof over his addition, and copied the style of the old chapel architecture. The only external alteration he had made had been the lowering of the sills of the windows.

It was in the furthest of these three rooms that Challis and his secretary worked, and it was from here that they saw the gloomy figure of the Rev. Percy Crashaw coming up the drive.

This was the third time he had called. His two former visits had been unrewarded, but that morning a letter had come from him, couched in careful phrases, the purport of which had been a request for an interview on a " matter of some moment."

Challis frowned, and rose from among an ordered litter of manuscripts.

" I shall have to see this man," he said to Lewes, and strode hastily out of the library.

Crashaw was perfunctorily apologetic, and Challis, looking somewhat out of place, smoking a heavy wooden pipe in the disused, bleak drawing-room, waited, almost silent, until his visitor should come to the point.

" . . . and the—er—matter of some moment, I mentioned," Crashaw mumbled on, " is, I should say, not altogether irrelevant to the work you are at present engaged upon."

" Indeed ! " commented Challis, with a lift of his thick eyebrows, " no Polynesians come to settle in Stoke, I trust ? "

" On broad lines, relevant on broad, anthropological lines, I mean," said Crashaw.

Challis grunted. " Go on ! " he said.

" You may remember that curious—er—abnormal child of the Stotts ? " asked Crashaw.

" Stotts ? Wait a minute. Yes ! Curious infant with an abnormally intelligent expression and the head of a hydrocephalic ? "

Crashaw nodded. " It's development has upset me in a most unusual way," he continued. " I must confess that I am entirely at a loss, and I really believe that you are the only person who can give me any intelligent assistance in the matter."

" Very good of you," murmured Challis.

" You see," said Crashaw, warming to his subject and interlacing his fingers, " I happen, by the merest accident, I may say, to be the child's godfather."

" Ah ! you have responsibilities ! " commented Challis, with the first glint of amusement in his eyes.

" I have," said Crashaw, " undoubtedly I have." He leaned forward with his hands still clasped together, and rested his forearms on his thighs. As he talked he worked his hands up and down from the wrists, by way of emphasis. " I am aware," he went on, " that on one point I can expect little sympathy from you, but I make an appeal to you, nevertheless, as a man of science and—and a magistrate ; for . . . for assistance."

He paused and looked up at Challis, received a nod of encouragement and developed his grievance.

" I want to have the child certified as an idiot, and sent to an asylum."

" On what grounds ? "

" He is undoubtedly lacking mentally," said Crashaw, " and his influence is, or may be, malignant."

" Explain," suggested Challis.

For a few seconds Crashaw paused, intent on the pattern of the carpet, and working his hands slowly. Challis saw that the man's knuckles were white, that he was straining his hands together.

" He has denied God," he said at last with great solemnity.

Challis rose abruptly, and went over to the window ; the next words were spoken to his back.

" I have, myself, heard this infant of four years use the most abhorrent blasphemy."

Challis had composed himself. " Oh ! I say ; that's bad," he said as he turned towards the room again.

Crashaw's head was still bowed. " And whatever may be your own philosophic doubts," he said, " I think you will agree with me that in such a case as this, something should be done. To me it is horrible, most horrible."

" Couldn't you give me any details ? " asked Challis.

" They are most repugnant to me," answered Crashaw.

" Quite, quite ! I understand. But if you want any assistance. . . . Or do you expect me to investigate ? "

" I thought it my duty, as his godfather, to see to the child's spiritual welfare," said Crashaw, ignoring the question put to him, " although he is not, now, one of my parishioners. I first went to Pym some few months ago, but the mother interposed between me and the child. I was not permitted to see him. It was not until a few weeks back that I met him —on the Common ; alone. Of course, I recognised him at once. He is quite unmistakable."

" And then ? " prompted Challis.

" I spoke to him, and he replied with, with—an abstracted air, without looking at me. He has not the appearance in any way of a normal child. I made a few ordinary remarks to him, and then I asked him if he knew his catechism. He replied that he did not know the word ' catechism.' I may mention that he speaks the dialect of the common people, but he has a much larger vocabulary. His mother has taught him to read, it appears."

" He seems to have a curiously apt intelligence," interpolated Challis.

Crashaw wrung his clasped hands and put the comment on one side. " I then spoke to him of some of the broad principles of the Church's teaching," he continued. " He listened quietly, without interruption, and when I stopped, he prompted me with questions."

" One minute ! " said Challis. " Tell me ; what sort of questions ?   That is most important."

" I do not remember precisely," returned Crashaw, " but one, I think, was as to the sources of the Bible. I did not read anything beyond simple and somewhat unusual curiosity into those questions, I may say. . . . I talked to him for some considerable time—I dare say for more than an hour. . . ."

" No signs of idiocy, apparently, during all this ? "

" I consider it less a case of idiocy than one of possession, maleficent possession," replied Crashaw. He did not see his host's grim smile.

" Well, and the blasphemy ? " prompted Challis.

" At the end of my instruction, the child, still looking away from me, shook his head and said that what I had told him was not true. I confess that

I was staggered. Possibly I lost my temper, somewhat. I may have grown rather warm in my speech. And at last . . . " Crashaw clenched his hands and spoke in such a low voice that Challis could hardly hear him. " At last he turned to me and said things which I could not possibly repeat, which I pray that I may never hear again from the mouth of any living being."

" Profanities, obscenities, er—swear-words," suggested Challis.

" Blasphemy, *blasphemy*," cried Crashaw. " Oh! I wonder that I did not injure the child."

Challis moved over to the window again. For more than a minute there was silence in that big, neglected-looking room. Then Crashaw's feelings began to find vent in words, in a long stream of insistent asseverations, pitched on a rising note that swelled into a diapason of indignation. He spoke of the position and power of his Church, of its influence for good among the uneducated, agricultural population among which he worked. He enlarged on the profound necessity for a living religion among the poorer classes ; and on the revolutionary tendency towards socialism, which would be encouraged if the great restraining power of a creed that enforced subservience to temporal power was once shaken. And, at last, he brought his arguments to a head by saying that the example of a child of four years old, openly defying a minister of the Church, and repudiating the very conception of the Deity, was an example which might produce a profound effect upon the minds of a slow-thinking people ; that such an example might be the leaven which would leaven the whole lump ; and that for the welfare of the whole neighbourhood it was an instant necessity that the child should be put under restraint, his tongue bridled, and any opportunity to proclaim his blasphemous doctrines forcibly denied to him. Long before he had concluded, Crashaw was on his feet, pacing the room, declaiming, waving his arms.

Challis stood, unanswering, by the window. He did not seem to hear ; he did not even shrug his shoulders. Not till Crashaw had brought his argument to a culmination, and boomed into a dramatic silence, did Challis turn and look at him.

" But you cannot confine a child in an asylum on those grounds," he said ; " the law does not permit it."

" The Church is above the law," replied Crashaw.

" Not in these days," said Challis ; " it is by law established ! "

Crashaw began to speak again, but Challis waved him down. " Quite, quite. I see your point," he said, " but I must see this child myself. Believe me, I will see what can be done. I will, at least,

try to prevent his spreading his opinions among the
yokels." He smiled grimly. " I quite agree with
you that that is a consummation which is not to be
desired."

" You will see him soon ? " asked Crashaw.

" To-day," returned Challis.

" And you will let me see you again, afterwards ? "

" Certainly."

Crashaw still hesitated for a moment. " I might,
perhaps, come with you," he ventured.

" On no account," said Challis.

II

Gregory Lewes was astonished at the long absence
of his chief ; he was more astonished when his chief
returned.

" I want you to come up with me to Pym, Lewes,"
said Challis ; " one of my tenants has been confound-
ing the rector of Stoke. It is a matter that must be
attended to."

Lewes was a fair-haired, hard-working young man,
with a bent for science in general that had not yet
crystallised into any special study. He had a
curious sense of humour, that proved something of
an obstacle in the way of specialisation. He did
not take Challis's speech seriously.

" Are you going as a magistrate ? " he asked ;
" or is it a matter for scientific investigation ? "

" Both," said Challis. " Come along ! "

" Are you serious, sir ? " Lewes still doubted.

" Intensely. I'll explain as we go," said Challis.

It is not more than a mile and a half from Challis
Court to Pym. The nearest way is by a cart track
through the beech woods, that winds up the hill to
the Common. In winter this track is almost im-
passable, over boot-top in heavy mud ; but the early
spring had been fairly dry, and Challis chose this
route.

As they walked, Challis went through the early
history of Victor Stott, so far as it was known to
him. " I had forgotten the child," he said; " I
thought it would die. You see, it is by way of being
an extraordinary freak of nature. It has, or had,
a curious look of intelligence. You must remember
that when I saw it, it was only a few months old.
But even then it conveyed in some inexplicable way
a sense of power. Every one felt it. There was
Harvey Walters, for instance—he vaccinated it ; I
made him confess that the child made him feel like
a school-boy. Only, you understand, it had not
spoken then——"

" What conveyed that sense of power ? " asked
Lewes.

" The way it had of looking at you, staring you
out of countenance, sizing you up and rejecting you.
It did that, I give you my word ; it did all that at a

few months old, and without the power of speech. Only, you see, I thought it was merely a freak of some kind, some abnormality that disgusted one in an unanalysed way. And I thought it would die. I certainly thought it would die. I am most eager to see this new development."

" I haven't heard. It confounded Crashaw, you say ? And it cannot be more than four or five years old now ? "

" Four ; four and a half," returned Challis, and then the conversation was interrupted by the necessity of skirting a tiny morass of wet leaf-mould that lay in a hollow.

" Confounded Crashaw ? I should think so," Challis went on, when they had found firm going again. " The good man would not soil his devoted tongue by any condescension to oratio recta, but I gathered that the child had made light of his divine authority."

" Great Cæsar ! " ejaculated Lewes ; " but that is immense. What did Crashaw do—shake him ? "

" No ; he certainly did not lay hands on him at all. His own expression was that he did not know how it was he did not do the child an injury. That is one of the things that interest me enormously. That power I spoke of must have been retained. Crashaw must have been blue with anger ; he could hardly repeat the story to me, he was so agitated.

It would have surprised me less if he had told me he had murdered the child. That I could have understood, perfectly."

" It is, of course, quite incomprehensible to me, as yet," commented Lewes.

When they came out of the woods on to the stretch of common from which you can see the great swelling undulations of the Hampden Hills, Challis stopped. A spear of April sunshine had pierced the load of cloud towards the west, and the bank of wood behind them gave shelter from the cold wind that had blown fiercely all the afternoon.

" It is a fine prospect," said Challis, with a sweep of his hand. " I sometimes feel, Lewes, that we are over-intent on our own little narrow interests. Here are you and I, busying ourselves in an attempt to throw some little light—a very little it must be—on some petty problems of the origin of our race. We are looking downwards, downwards always ; digging in old muck-heaps ; raking up all kinds of unsavoury rubbish to prove that we are born out of the dirt. And we have never a thought for the future in all our work,—a future that may be glorious, who knows ? Here, perhaps in this village, insignificant from most points of view, but set in a country that should teach us to raise our eyes from the ground ; here, in this tiny hamlet, is living a child who may become a greater than Socrates or

Shakespeare, a child who may revolutionise our conceptions of time and space. There have been great men in the past who have done that, Lewes; there is no reason for us to doubt that still greater men may succeed them."

"No; there is no reason for us to doubt that," said Lewes, and they walked on in silence towards the Stotts' cottage.

III

Challis knocked and walked in. They found Ellen Mary and her son at the tea-table.

The mother rose to her feet and dropped a respectful curtsy. The boy glanced once at Gregory Lewes and then continued his meal as if he were unaware of any strange presence in the room.

"I'm sorry. I am afraid we are interrupting you," Challis apologised. "Pray sit down, Mrs. Stott, and go on with your tea."

"Thank you, sir. I'd just finished, sir," said Ellen Mary, and remained standing with an air of quiet deference.

Challis took the celebrated armchair, and motioned Lewes to the window-sill, the nearest available seat for him. "Please sit down, Mrs. Stott," he said, and Ellen Mary sat, apologetically.

The boy pushed his cup towards his mother, and

pointed to the teapot ; he made a grunting sound to attract her attention.

" You'll excuse me, sir," murmured Ellen Mary, and she refilled the cup and passed it back to her son, who received it without any acknowledgment. Challis and Lewes were observing the boy intently, but he took not the least notice of their scrutiny. He discovered no trace of self-consciousness ; Henry Challis and Gregory Lewes appeared to have no place in the world of his abstraction.

The figure the child presented to his two observers was worthy of careful scrutiny.

At the age of four and a half years, the Wonder was bald, save for a few straggling wisps of reddish hair above the ears and at the base of the skull, and a weak, sparse down, of the same colour, on the crown. The eyebrows, too, were not marked by any line of hair, but the eyelashes were thick, though short, and several shades darker than the hair on the skull.

The face is not so easily described. The mouth and chin were relatively small, overshadowed by that broad cliff of forehead, but they were firm, the chin well moulded, the lips thin and compressed. The nose was unusual when seen in profile. There was no sign of a bony bridge, but it was markedly curved and jutted out at a curious angle from the line of the face. The nostrils were wide and open. None

of these features produced any effect of childishness ;
but this effect was partly achieved by the contours
of the cheeks, and by the fact that there was no
indication of any lines on the face.

The eyes nearly always wore their usual expression
of abstraction. It was very rarely that the Wonder
allowed his intelligence to be exhibited by that
medium. When he did, the effect was strangely
disconcerting, blinding. One received an impression of extraordinary concentration : it was as though
for an instant the boy was able to give one a glimpse
of the wonderful force of his intellect. When he
looked one in the face with intention, and suddenly
allowed one to realise, as it were, all the dominating
power of his brain, one shrank into insignificance,
one felt as an ignorant, intelligent man may feel
when confronted with some elaborate theorem of
the higher mathematics. " Is it possible that any
one can really understand these things ? " such a
man might think with awe, and in the same way one
apprehended some vast, inconceivable possibilities
of mind-function when the Wonder looked at one
with, as I have said, intention.

He was dressed in a little jacket-suit, and wore a
linen collar ; the knickerbockers, loose and badly
cut, fell a little below the knees. His stockings were
of worsted, his boots clumsy and thick-soled, though
relatively tiny. One had the impression always that

his body was fragile and small, but as a matter of fact the body and limbs were, if anything, slightly better developed than those of the average child of four and a half years.

Challis had ample opportunity to make these observations at various periods. He began them as he sat in the Stotts' cottage. At first he did not address the boy directly.

" I hear your son has been having a religious controversy with Mr. Crashaw," was his introduction to the object of his visit.

" Indeed, sir ! " Plainly this was not news to Mrs. Stott.

" Your son told you ? " suggested Challis.

" Oh ! no, sir, 'e never told me," replied Mrs. Stott, " 'twas Mr. Crashaw. 'E's been 'ere several times lately."

Challis looked sharply at the boy, but he gave no sign that he heard what was passing.

" Yes; Mr. Crashaw seems rather upset about it."

" I'm sorry, sir, but—— "

" Yes; speak plainly," prompted Challis. " I assure you, that you will have no cause to regret any confidence you may make to me."

" I can't see as it's any business of Mr. Crashaw's, sir, if you'll forgive me for sayin' so."

" He has been worrying you ? "

" 'E 'as, sir, but 'e . . . " she glanced at her son—

9

she laid a stress on the pronoun always when she
spoke of him that differentiated its significance—
" 'e 'asn't seen Mr. Crashaw again, sir."

Challis turned to the boy. " You are not interested in Mr. Crashaw, I suppose ? " he asked.

The boy took no notice of the question.

Challis was piqued. If this extraordinary child
really had an intelligence, surely it must be possible
to appeal to that intelligence in some way. He
made another effort, addressing Mrs. Stott.

" I think we must forgive Mr. Crashaw, you know,
Mrs. Stott. As I understand it, your boy at the age
of four years and a half has defied—his cloth, if I
may say so." He paused, and as he received no
answer, continued : " But I hope that matter may
be easily arranged."

" Thank you, sir," said Mrs. Stott. " It's very
kind of you. I'm sure, I'm greatly obliged to you,
sir."

" That's only one reason of my visit to you,
however." Challis hesitated. " I've been wondering whether I might not be able to help you and your
son in some other way. I understand that he has
unusual power of—of intelligence."

" Indeed 'e 'as, sir," responded Mrs. Stott.

" And he can read, can't he ? "

" I've learned 'im what I could, sir : it isn't much."

" Well, perhaps I could lend him a few books."

Challis made a significant pause, and again he looked at the boy ; but there was no response, so he continued : " Tell me what he has read."

" We've no books, sir, and we never 'ardly see a paper now. All we 'ave in the 'ouse is a Bible and two copies of Lillywhite's cricket annual as my 'usband left be'ind."

Challis smiled. " Has he read those ? " he asked.

" The Bible 'e 'as, I believe," replied Mrs. Stott.

It was a conversation curious in its impersonality. Challis was conscious of the anomaly that he was speaking in the boy's presence, crediting him with a remarkable intelligence, and yet addressing a frankly ignorant woman as though the boy was not in the room. Yet how could he break that deliberate silence ? It seemed to him as though there must, after all, be some mistake ; yet how account for Crashaw's story if the boy were indeed an idiot ?

With a slight show of temper he turned to the Wonder.

" Do you want to read ? " he asked. " I have between forty and fifty thousand books in my library. I think it possible that you might find one or two which would interest you."

The Wonder lifted his hand as though to ask for silence. For a minute, perhaps, no one spoke. All waited, expectant ; Challis and Lewes with intent eyes fixed on the detached expression of the child's face, Ellen Mary with bent head. It was a strange, yet very logical question that came at last :

" What should I learn out of all them books ? " asked the Wonder. He did not look at Challis as he spoke.

IV

Challis drew a deep breath and looked at Lewes. " A difficult question, that, Lewes," he said.

Lewes lifted his eyebrows and pulled at his fair moustache. " If you take the question literally," he muttered.

" You might learn—the essential part . . . of all the knowledge that has been . . . discovered by mankind," said Challis. He phrased his sentence carefully, as though he were afraid of being trapped.

" Should I learn what I am ? " asked the Wonder.

Challis understood the question in its metaphysical acceptation. He had the sense of a powerful but undirected intelligence working from the simple premisses of experience ; of a cloistered mind that had functioned profoundly ; a mind unbound by the tradition of all the speculations and discoveries of man, the essential conclusions of which were contained in that library at Challis Court.

" No ! " said Challis, after a perceptible interval,

" that you will not learn from any books in my possession, but you will find grounds for speculation."

" Grounds for speculation ? " questioned the Wonder. He repeated the words quite clearly.

" Material—matter from which you can—er—formulate theories of your own," explained Challis.

The Wonder shook his head. It was evident that Challis's sentence conveyed little or no meaning to him.

He got down from his chair and took up an old cricket cap of his father's, a cap which his mother had let out by the addition of another gore of cloth that did not match the original material. He pulled this cap carefully over his bald head, and then made for the door.

At the threshold the strange child paused, and without looking at any one present said : " I'll coom to your library," and went out.

Challis joined Lewes at the window, and they watched the boy make his deliberate way along the garden path and up the lane towards the fields beyond.

" You let him go out by himself ? " asked Challis.

" He likes to be in the air, sir," replied Ellen Mary.

" I suppose you have to let him go his own way ? "

" Oh ! yes, sir."

" I will send the governess cart up for him to-morrow morning," said Challis, " at ten o'clock. That is, of course, if you have no objection to his coming."

"'E said 'e'd coom, sir," replied Ellen Mary. Her tone implied that there was no appeal possible against her son's statement of his wishes.

V

" His methods do not lack terseness," remarked Lewes, when he and Challis were out of earshot of the cottage.

" His methods and manners are damnable," said Challis, " but——"

" You were going to say ? " prompted Lewes.

" Well, what is your opinion ? "

" I am not convinced, as yet," said Lewes.

" Oh, surely," expostulated Challis.

" Not from objective, personal evidence. Let us put Crashaw out of our minds for the moment."

" Very well ; go on, state your case."

" He has, so far, made four remarks in our presence," said Lewes, gesticulating with his walking stick. " Two of them can be neglected; his repetition of your words, which he did not understand, and his condescending promise to study your library."

" Yes ; I'm with you, so far."

" Now, putting aside the preconception with which we entered the cottage, was there really anything in the other two remarks ? Were they not the type of simple, unreasoning questions which one may often hear from the mouth of a child of that age ? ' What shall I learn from your books ? ' Well, it is the natural question of the ignorant child, who has no conception of the contents of books, no experience which would furnish material for his imagination."

" Well ? "

" The second remark is more explicable still. It is a remark we all make in childhood, in some form or another. I remember quite well at the age of six or seven asking my mother : ' Which is me, my soul or my body ? ' I was brought up on the Church catechism. But you at once accepted these questions—which, I maintain, were questions possible in the mouth of a simple, ignorant child—in some deep, metaphysical acceptation. Don't you think, sir, we should wait for further evidence before we attribute any phenomenal intelligence to this child ? "

" Quite the right attitude to take, Lewes—the scientific attitude," replied Challis. " Let's go by the lane," he added, as they reached the entrance to the wood.

For some few minutes they walked in silence ; Challis with his head down, his heavy shoulders humped. His hands were clasped behind him, dragging his stick as it were a tail, which he occasionally cocked. He walked with a little stumble now and again, his eyes on the ground. Lewes strode with a sure foot, his head up, and he slashed at the tangle of last year's growth on the bank whenever he passed some tempting butt for the sword-play of his stick.

" Do you think, then," said Challis at last, " that much of the atmosphere—you must have marked the atmosphere—of the child's personality, was a creation of our own minds, due to our preconceptions ? "

" Yes, I think so," Lewes replied, a touch of defiance in his tone.

" Isn't that what you *want* to believe ? " asked Challis.

Lewes hit at a flag of dead bracken and missed. " You mean . . . ? " he prevaricated.

" I mean that that is a much stronger influence than any preconception, my dear Lewes. I'm no pragmatist, as you know ; but there can be no doubt that with the majority of us the wish to believe a thing is true constitutes the truth of that thing for us. And that is, in my opinion, the wrong attitude for either scientist or philosopher. Now, in the case we are discussing, I suppose, at bottom I should like to agree with you. One does not like to feel that a child of four and a half has greater intellectual powers than oneself. Candidly, I do not like it at all.''

"Of course not ! But I can't think that——"

"You can if you try; you would at once if you wished to,'' returned Challis, anticipating the completion of Lewes's sentence.

"I'll admit that there are some remarkable facts in the case of this child," said Lewes, "but I do not see why we should, as yet, take the whole proposition for granted.''

"No! I am with you there," returned Challis. And no more was said until they were nearly home.

Just before they turned into the drive, however, Challis stopped. "Do you know, Lewes," he said, "I am not sure that I am doing a wise thing in bringing that child here ! ''

Lewes did not understand. "No, sir ? Why not ? '' he asked.

"Why, think of the possibilities of that child, if he has all the powers I credit him with," said Challis. "Think of his possibilities for original thought if he is kept away from all the traditions of this futile learning.'' He waved an arm in the direction of the elongated chapel.

"Oh! but surely," remonstrated Lewes, "that is a necessary groundwork. Knowledge is built up step by step.''

"Is it ? I wonder. I sometimes doubt," said

Challis. " Yes, I sometimes doubt whether we have ever learned anything at all that is worth knowing. And, perhaps, this child, if he were kept away from books. . . . However, the thing is done now, and in any case he would never have been able to dodge the School attendance officer."

CHAPTER VIII

HIS FIRST VISIT TO CHALLIS COURT

I

"Shall you be able to help me in collating your notes of the Tikopia observations this morning, sir?" Lewes asked. He rose from the breakfast-table and lit a cigarette. There was no ceremony between Challis and his secretary.

"You forget our engagement for ten o'clock," said Challis.

"Need that distract us?"

"It need not, but doesn't it seem to you that it may furnish us with valuable material?"

"Hardly pertinent, sir, is it?"

"What line do you think of taking up, Lewes?" asked Challis with apparent irrelevance.

"With regard to this—this phenomenon?"

"No, no. I was speaking of your own ambitions." Challis had sauntered over to the window; he stood, with his back to Lewes, looking out at the blue and white of the April sky.

Lewes frowned. He did not understand the gist of the question. "I suppose there is a year's work on this book before me yet," he said.

"Quite, quite," replied Challis, watching a cloud shadow swarm up the slope of Deane Hill. "Yes, certainly a year's work. I was thinking of the future."

"I have thought of laboratory work in connection with psychology," said Lewes, still puzzled.

"I thought I remembered your saying something of the kind," murmured Challis absently. "We are going to have more rain. It will be a late spring this year."

"Had the question any bearing on our engagement of this morning?" Lewes was a little anxious, uncertain whether this inquiry as to his future had not some particular significance; a hint, perhaps, that his services would not be required much longer.

"Yes; I think it had," said Challis. "I saw the governess cart go up the road a few minutes since."

"I suppose the boy will be here in a quarter of an hour?" said Lewes by way of keeping up the conversation. He was puzzled; he did not know Challis in this mood. He did not conceive it possible that Challis could be nervous about the arrival of so insignificant a person as this Stott child.

"It's all very ridiculous," broke out Challis suddenly; and he turned away from the window, and joined Lewes by the fire. " Don't you think so ? "

" I'm afraid I don't follow you, sir."

Challis laughed. " I'm not surprised," he said; " I was a trifle inconsecutive. But I wish you were more interested in this child, Lewes. The thought of him engrosses me, and yet I don't want to meet him. I should be relieved to hear that he wasn't coming. Surely you, as a student of psychology . . . " he broke off with a lift of his heavy shoulders.

" Oh ! Yes ! I *am* interested, certainly, as you say, as a student of psychology. We ought to take some measurements. The configuration of the skull is not abnormal otherwise than in its relation to the development of the rest of his body, but . . . " Lewes meandered off into somewhat abstruse speculation with regard to the significance of craniology.

Challis nodded his head and murmured : " Quite, quite," occasionally. He seemed glad that Lewes should continue to talk.

The lecture was interrupted by the appearance of the governess cart.

" By Jove, he *has* come," ejaculated Challis in the middle of one of Lewes's periods. " You'll have to see me through this, my boy. I'm damned if I know how to take the child."

Lewes flushed, annoyed at the interruption of his

lecture. He had believed that he had been interesting. "Curse the kid," was the thought in his
mind as he followed Challis to the window.

II

Jessop, the groom deputed to fetch the Wonder
from Pym, looked a little uneasy, perhaps a little
scared. When he drew up at the porch, the child
pointed to the door of the cart and indicated that
it was to be opened for him. He was evidently used
to being waited upon. When this command had
been obeyed, he descended deliberately and then
pointed to the front door.

"Open!" he said clearly, as Jessop hesitated.
The Wonder knew nothing of bells or ceremony.

Jessop came down from the cart and rang.

The butler opened the door. He was an old
servant and accustomed to his master's eccentrici-
ties, but he was not prepared for the vision of that
strange little figure, with a large head in a parti-
coloured cricket-cap, an apparition that immediately
walked straight by him into the hall, and pointed
to the first door he came to.

"Oh, dear! Well, to be sure," gasped Heathcote.
"Why, whatever——"

"Open!" commanded the Wonder, and Heathcote obeyed, weak-kneed.

The door chanced to be the right one, the door of the breakfast-room, and the Wonder walked in, still wearing his cap.

Challis came forward to meet him with a conventional greeting. " I'm glad you were able to come . . . " he began, but the child took no notice ; he looked rapidly round the room, and not finding what he wanted, signified his desire by a single word.

" Books," he said, and looked at Challis.

Heathcote stood at the door, hesitating between amazement and disapproval. " I've never seen the like," was how he phrased his astonishment later, in the servants' hall, " never in all my born days. To see that melon-'eaded himp in a cricket-cap hordering the master about. Well, there——"

" Jessop says he fair got the creeps drivin' 'im over," said the cook. " 'E says the child's not right in 'is 'ead."

Much embroidery followed in the servants' hall.

INTERLUDE

THIS brief history of the Hampdenshire Wonder is marked by a stereotyped division into three parts, an arbitrary arrangement dependent on the experience of the writer. The true division becomes manifest at this point. The life of Victor Stott was cut into two distinct sections, between which there is no correlation. The first part should tell the story of his mind during the life of experience, the time occupied in observation of the phenomena of life presented to him in fact, without any specific teaching on the theories of existence and progress, or on the speculation as to ultimate destiny. The second part should deal with his entry into the world of books ; into that account of a long series of collated experiments and partly verified hypotheses we call science ; into the imperfectly developed system of inductive and deductive logic which determines mathematics and philosophy ; into the long, inaccurate and largely unverifiable account of human blindness and error known as history ; and into the realm of idealism, symbol, and pitiful pride we find in the story of poetry, letters, and religion.

I will confess that I once contemplated the writing of such a history.   It was Challis who, in his courtly, gentle way, pointed out to me that no man living had the intellectual capacity to undertake so profound a work.

For some three months before I had this conversation with Challis, I had been wrapped in solitude, dreaming, speculating.   I had been uplifted in thought, I had come to believe myself inspired as a result of my separation from the world of men, and of the deep introspection and meditation in which I had been plunged.   I had arrived at a point, perhaps not far removed from madness, at which I thought myself capable of setting out the true history of Victor Stott.

Challis broke the spell.   He cleared away the false glamour which was blinding and intoxicating me, and brought me back to a condition of open-eyed sanity.   To Challis I owe a great debt.

Yet at the moment I was sunk in depression.   All the glory of my vision had faded ; the afterglow was quenched in the blackness of the night that drew out of the east and fell from the zenith as a curtain of utter darkness.

Again Challis came to my rescue.   He brought me a great sheaf of notes.

" Look here," he said, " if you can't write a true history of that strange child, I see no reason why

you should not write his story as it is known to you,
as it impinges on your own life. After all, you, in
many ways, know more of him than any one. You
came nearest to receiving his confidence."

" But only during the last few months," I said.

" Does that matter ? " said Challis with an up-
heaval of his shoulders—" shrug " is far too insignificant a word for that mountainous humping.
" Is any biography founded on better material
than you have at command ? "

He unfolded his bundle of notes. " See here," he
said, " here is some magnificent material for you—
first-hand observations made at the time. Can't
you construct a story from that ? "

Even then I began to cast my story in a slightly
biographical form. I wrote half a dozen chapters,
and read them to Challis.

" Magnificent, my dear fellow," was his comment,
" magnificent; but no one will believe it."

I had been carried away by my own prose, and
with the natural vanity of the author, I resented
intensely his criticism.

For some weeks I did not see Challis again, and I
persisted in my futile endeavour, but always as I
wrote that killing suggestion insinuated itself : " No
one will believe you." At times I felt as a man
may feel who has spent many years in a lunatic
asylum, and after his release is for ever engaged

in a struggle to allay the doubts of a leering suspicion.

I gave up the hopeless task at last, and sought out Challis again.

" Write it as a story," he suggested, " and give up the attempt to carry conviction."

And in that spirit, adopting the form of a story, I did begin, and in that form I hope to finish.

But here as I reach the great division, the determining factor of Victor Stott's life, I am constrained to pause and apologise. I have become uncomfortably conscious of my own limitations, and the feeble, ephemeral methods I am using. I am trifling with a wonderful story, embroidering my facts with the tawdry detail of my own imagining.

I saw—I see—no other way.

This is, indeed, a preface, yet I prefer to put it in this place, since it was at this time I wrote it.

.   .   .   .   .

On the Common a faint green is coming again like a mist among the ash-trees, while the oak is still dead and bare.   Last year the oak came first.

They say we shall have a wet summer.

PART II (*continued*)

THE WONDER AMONG BOOKS

CHAPTER IX

HIS PASSAGE THROUGH THE PRISON OF
KNOWLEDGE

I

CHALLIS led the way to the library ; Lewes, petulant
and mutinous, hung in the rear.

The Wonder toddled forward, unabashed, to enter
his new world. On the threshold, however, he
paused. His comprehensive stare took in a sweep-
ing picture of enclosing walls of books, and beyond
was a vista of further rooms, of more walls all lined
from floor to ceiling with records of human discovery,
endeavour, doubt, and hope.

The Wonder stayed and stared. Then he took
two faltering steps into the room and stopped again,
and, finally, he looked up at Challis with doubt and
question ; his gaze no longer quelling and authorita-
tive, but hesitating, compliant, perhaps a little
childlike.

" 'Ave you read all these ? " he asked.

It was a curious picture. The tall figure of Challis, stooping, as always, slightly forward; Challis, with his seaman's eyes and scholar's head, his hands loosely clasped together behind his back, paying such scrupulous attention to that grotesque representative of a higher intellectuality, clothed in the dress of a villager, a patched cricket-cap drawn down over his globular skull, his little arms hanging loosely at his sides; who, nevertheless, even in this new, strange aspect of unwonted humility bore on his face the promise of some ultimate development which differentiated him from all other humanity, as the face of humanity is differentiated from the face of its prognathous ancestor.

The scene is set in a world of books, and in the background lingers the athletic figure and fair head of Lewes, the young Cambridge undergraduate, the disciple of science, hardly yet across the threshold which divides him from the knowledge of his own ignorance.

" 'Ave you read all these ? " asked the Wonder.

" A greater part of them—in effect," replied Challis. " There is much repetition, you understand, and much record of experiment which becomes, in a sense, worthless when the conclusions are either finally accepted or rejected."

The eyes of the Wonder shifted and their expression became abstracted; he seemed to lose consciousness of the outer world; he wore the look which you may see in the eyes of Jakob Schlesinger's portrait of the mature Hegel, a look of profound introspection and analysis.

There was an interval of silence, and then the Wonder unknowingly gave expression to a quotation from Hamlet. " Words," he whispered reflectively, and then again " words."

II

Challis understood him. " You have not yet learned the meaning of words ? " he asked.

The brief period—the only one recorded—of amazement and submission was over. It may be that he had doubted during those few minutes of time whether he was well advised to enter into that world of books, whether he would not by so doing stunt his own mental growth. It may be that the decision of so momentous a question should have been postponed for a year—two years ; to a time when his mind should have had further possibilities for unlettered expansion. However that may be, he decided now and finally. He walked to the table and climbed up on a chair.

" Books about words," he commanded, and pointed at Challis and Lewes.

They brought him the latest production of the

twentieth century in many volumes, the work of a dozen eminent authorities on the etymology of the English language, and they seated him on eight volumes of the *Encyclopædia Britannica* (India paper edition) in order that he might reach the level of the table.

At first they tried to show him how his wonderful dictionary should be used, but he pushed them on one side, neither then nor at any future time would he consent to be taught—the process was too tedious for him, his mind worked more fluently, rapidly, and comprehensively than the mind of the most gifted teacher that could have been found for him.

So Challis and Lewes stood on one side and watched him, and he was no more embarrassed by their presence than if they had been in another world, as, possibly, they were.

He began with volume one, and he read the title page and the introduction, the list of abbreviations, and all the preliminary matter in due order.

Challis noted that when the Wonder began to read, he read no faster than the average educated man, but that he acquired facility at a most astounding rate, and that when he had been reading for a few days his eye swept down the column, as it were at a single glance.

Challis and Lewes watched him for, perhaps, half an hour, and then, seeing that their presence was of an entirely negligible value to the Wonder, they left him and went into the farther room.

" Well ? " asked Challis, " what do you make of him ? "

" Is he reading or pretending to read ? " parried Lewes. " Do you think it possible that he could read so fast ? Moreover, remember thathe has admitted that he knows few words of the English language, yet he does not refer from volume to volume ; he does not look up the meanings of the many unknown words which must occur in every definition."

" I know. I had noticed that."

" Then you think he *is* humbugging—pretending to read ? "

" No ; that solution seems to me altogether unlikely. He could not, for one thing, simulate that look of attention. Remember, Lewes, the child is not yet five years old."

" What is your explanation, then ? "

" I am wondering whether the child has not a memory beside which the memory of a Macaulay would appear insignificant."

Lewes did not grasp Challis's intention. " Even so . . . " he began.

" And," continued Challis, " I am wondering whether, if that is the case, he is, in effect, prepared to learn the whole dictionary by heart, and, so to speak, collate its contents later, in his mind."

"Oh! Sir!" Lewes smiled. The supposition was too outrageous to be taken seriously. "Surely, you can't mean that." There was something in Lewes's tone which carried a hint of contempt for so far-fetched a hypothesis.

Challis was pacing up and down the library, his hands clasped behind him. "Yes, I mean it," he said, without looking up. "I put it forward as a serious theory, worthy of full consideration."

Lewes sneered. "Oh, surely not, sir," he said.

Challis stopped and faced him. "Why not, Lewes; why not?" he asked, with a kindly smile. "Think of the gap which separates your intellectual powers from those of a Polynesian savage. Why, after all, should it be impossible that this child's powers should equally transcend our own? A freak, if you will, an abnormality, a curious effect of nature's, like the giant puff-ball—but still——"

"Oh! yes, sir, I grant you the thing is not impossible from a theoretical point of view," argued Lewes, "but I think you are theorising on altogether insufficient evidence. I am willing to admit that such a freak is theoretically possible, but I have not yet found the indications of such a power in the child."

Challis resumed his pacing. "Quite, quite," he

assented; " your method is perfectly correct—perfectly correct. We must wait."

At twelve o'clock Challis brought a glass of milk and some biscuits, and set them beside the Wonder —he was at the letter " B."

" Well, how are you getting on ? " asked Challis.

The Wonder took not the least notice of the question, but he stretched out a little hand and took a biscuit and ate it, without looking up from his reading.

" I wish he'd answer questions," Challis remarked to Lewes, later.

" I should prescribe a sound shaking," returned Lewes.

Challis smiled. " Well, see here, Lewes," he said, " I'll take the responsibility ; you go and experiment, go and shake him."

Lewes looked through the folding doors at the picture of the Wonder, intent on his study of the great dictionary. " Since you've franked me," he said, " I'll do it—but not now. I'll wait till he gives me some occasion."

" Good," replied Challis, " my offer holds . . . and, by the way, I have no doubt that an occasion will present itself. Doesn't it strike you as likely, Lewes, that we shall see a good deal of the child here ? "

They stood for some minutes, watching the picture

of that intent student, framed in the written thoughts of his predecessors.

III

The Wonder ignored an invitation to lunch ; he ignored, also, the tray that was sent in to him. He read on steadily till a quarter to six, by which time he was at the end of " L," and then he climbed down from his Encyclopædia, and made for the door. Challis, working in the farther room, saw him and came out to open the door.

" Are you going now ? " he asked.

The child nodded.

" I will order the cart for you, if you will wait ten minutes," said Challis.

The child shook his head. " It's very necessary to have air," he said.

Something in the tone and pronunciation struck Challis, and awoke a long dormant memory. The sentence spoken, suddenly conjured up a vision of the Stotts' cottage at Stoke, of the Stotts at tea, of a cradle in the shadow, and of himself, sitting in an uncomfortable armchair and swinging his stick between his knees. When the child had gone— walking deliberately, and evidently regarding the mile-and-a-half walk through the twilight wood and over the deserted Common as a trivial incident in the day's business—Challis set himself to analyse that curious association.

As he strolled back across the hall to the library, he tried to reconstruct the scene of the cottage at Stoke, and to recall the outline of the conversation he had had with the Stotts.

"Lewes!" he said, when he reached the room in which his secretary was working, "Lewes, this is curious," and he described the associations called up by the child's speech. "The curious thing is," he continued, "that I had gone to advise Mrs. Stott to take a cottage at Pym, because the Stoke villagers were hostile, in some way, and she did not care to take the child out in the street. It is more than probable that I used just those words, 'It is very necessary to have air,' very probable. Now, what about my memory theory? The child was only six months old at that time."

Lewes appeared unconvinced. "There is nothing very unusual in the sentence," he said.

"Forgive me," replied Challis, "I don't agree with you. It is not phrased as a villager would phrase it, and, as I tell you, it was not spoken with the local accent."

"You may have spoken the sentence to-day," suggested Lewes.

"I may, of course, though I don't remember saying anything of the sort, but that would not account for the curiously vivid association which was conjured up."

Lewes pursed his lips. " No, no, no," he said. " But that is hardly ground for argument, is it ? "

" I suppose not," returned Challis thoughtfully; " but when you take up psychology, Lewes, I should much like you to specialise in a careful inquiry into association in connection with memory. I feel certain that if one can reproduce, as nearly as may be, any complex sensation one has experienced, no matter how long ago, one will stimulate what I may call an abnormal memory of all the associations connected with that experience. Just now I saw the interior of that room in the Stotts' cottage so clearly that I had an image of a dreadful oleograph of Disraeli hanging on the wall. But, now, I cannot for the life of me remember whether there was such an oleograph or not. I do not remember noticing it at the time."

" Yes, that's very interesting," replied Lewes. " There is certainly a wide field for research in that direction."

" You might throw much light on our mental processes," replied Challis.

(It was as the outcome of this conversation that Gregory Lewes did, two years afterwards, take up this line of study. The only result up to the present time is his little brochure *Reflexive Associations*, which has hardly added to our knowledge of the subject.)

IV

Challis's anticipation that he and Lewes would be greatly favoured by the Wonder's company was fully realised.

The child put in an appearance at half-past nine the next morning, just as the governess cart was starting out to fetch him. When he was admitted he went straight to the library, climbed on to the chair, upon which the volumes of the Encyclopædia still remained, and continued his reading where he had left off on the previous evening.

He read steadily throughout the day without giving utterance to speech of any kind.

Challis and Lewes went out in the afternoon, and left the child deep in study. They came in at five o'clock, and went to the library. The Wonder, however, was not there.

Challis rang the bell.

" Has little Stott gone ? " he asked when Heathcote came.

" I 'aven't seen 'im, sir," said Heathcote.

" Just find out if any one opened the door for him, will you ? " said Challis. " He couldn't possibly have opened that door for himself."

II

" No one 'asn't let Master Stott hout, sir," Heathcote reported on his return.

" Are you sure ? "

" Quite sure, sir. I've made full hinquiries," said
Heathcote with dignity.

" Well, we'd better find him," said Challis.

" The window is open," suggested Lewes.

" He would hardly . . . " began Challis, walking
over to the low sill of the open window, but he broke
off in his sentence and continued, " By Jove, he did,
though ; look here ! "

It was, indeed, quite obvious that the Wonder had
made his exit by the window ; the tiny prints of his
feet were clearly marked in the mould of the flower-
bed ; he had, moreover, disregarded all results of
early spring floriculture.

" See how he has smashed those daffodils," said
Lewes. " What an infernally cheeky little brute he
is ! "

" What interests me is the logic of the child,"
returned Challis. " I would venture to guess that
he wasted no time in trying to attract attention.
The door was closed, so he just got out of the
window. I rather admire the spirit ; there is something Napoleonic about him. Don't you think so ? "

Lewes shrugged his shoulders. Heathcote's expression was quite non-committal.

" You'd better send Jessop up to Pym, Heath-

cote," said Challis.   " Let him find out whether the
child is safe at home."

Jessop reported an hour afterwards that Master
Stott had arrived home quite safely, and Mrs. Stott
was much obliged.

v

" What can I give that child to read to-day ? "
asked Challis at breakfast next morning.

" I should reverse the arrangement ; let him sit
on the Dictionary and read the Encyclopædia."
Lewes always approached the subject of the Wonder
with a certain supercilious contempt.

" You are not convinced yet that he isn't humbugging ? "

" No ! Frankly, I'm not."

" Well, well, we must wait for more evidence,
before we argue about it," said Challis, but they sat
on over the breakfast-table, waiting for the child to
put in an appearance, and their conversation hovered
over the topic of his intelligence.

" Half-past ten ? " Challis ejaculated at last, with
surprise. " We are getting into slack habits,
Lewes."   He rose and rang the bell.

" Apparently the Stott infant has had enough of
it," suggested Lewes. " Perhaps he has exhausted
the interest of dictionary illustrations."

" We shall see," replied Challis, and then to a

deferentially appearing Heathcote he said : " Has Master Stott come this morning ? "

" No, sir. Leastways, no one 'asn't let 'im in, sir."

" It may be that he is mentally collating the results of the past two days' reading," said Challis, as he and Lewes made their way to the library.

" Oh ! " was all Lewes's reply, but it conveyed much of impatient contempt for his employer's attitude.

Challis only smiled.

When they entered the library they found the Wonder hard at work, and he had, of his own initiative, adopted the plan ironically suggested by Lewes, for he had succeeded in transferring the Dictionary volumes to the chair, and he was deep in volume one, of the eleventh edition of the *Encyclopædia Britannica.*

The library was never cleared up by any one except Challis or his deputy, but an early housemaid had been sent to dust, and she had left the casement of one of the lower lights of the window open. The means of the Wonder's entrance was thus clearly in evidence.

" It's Napoleonic," murmured Challis.

" It's most infernal cheek," returned Lewes in a loud voice, " I should not be at all surprised if that promised shaking were not administered to-day."

The Wonder took no notice. Challis says that on that morning his eyes were travelling down the page at about the rate at which one could count the lines.

" He isn't reading," said Lewes. " No one could read as fast as that, and most certainly not a child of four and a half."

" If he would only answer questions . . . " hesitated Challis.

" Oh ! of course he won't do that," said Lewes. " He's clever enough not to give himself away."

The two men went over to the table and looked down over the child's shoulder. He was in the middle of the article on algebra.

Lewes made a gesture. " Now do you believe he's humbugging ? " he asked confidently, and made no effort to modulate his voice.

Challis drew his eyebrows together. " My boy," he said, and laid his hand lightly on Victor Stott's shoulder, " can you understand what you are reading there ? "

But no answer was vouchsafed. Challis sighed. " Come along, Lewes," he said ; " we must waste no more time."

Lewes wore a look of smug triumph as they went to the farther room, but he was clever enough to refrain from expressing his triumph in speech.

VI

Challis gave directions that the window which the Wonder had found to be his most convenient method of entry and exit should be kept open, except at night; and a stool was placed under the sill inside the room, and a low bench was fixed outside to facilitate the child's goings and comings. Also, a little path was made across the flower-bed.

The Wonder gave no trouble. He arrived at nine o'clock every morning, Sunday included, and left at a quarter to six in the evening. On wet days he was provided with a waterproof which had evidently been made by his mother out of a larger garment. This he took off when he entered the room and left on the stool under the window.

He was given a glass of milk and a plate of bread-and-butter at twelve o'clock; and except for this he demanded and received no attention.

For three weeks he devoted himself exclusively to the study of the Encyclopædia.

Lewes was puzzled.

Challis spoke little of the child during these three weeks, but he often stood at the entrance to the farther rooms and watched the Wonder's eyes travelling so rapidly yet so intently down the page. That sight had a curious fascination for him; he returned to his own work by an effort, and an hour afterwards he would be back again at the door of the larger room. Sometimes Lewes would hear him mutter: "If he would only answer a few questions. . . ." There was always one hope in Challis's mind. He hoped that some sort of climax might be reached when the Encyclopædia was finished. The child must, at least, ask then for another book. Even if he chose one for himself, his choice might furnish some sort of a test.

So Challis waited and said little ; and Lewes was puzzled, because he was beginning to doubt whether it were possible that the child could sustain a pose so long. That, in itself, would be evidence of extraordinary abnormality. Lewes fumbled in his mind for another hypothesis.

This reading craze may be symptomatic of some form of idiocy, was his thought ; " and I don't believe he does read," was the inevitable rider.

Mrs. Stott usually came to meet her son, and sometimes she would come early in the afternoon and stand at the window watching him at his work ; but neither Challis nor Lewes ever saw the Wonder display by any sign that he was aware of his mother's presence.

During those three weeks the Wonder held himself completely detached from any intercourse with the world of men. At the end of that period he once more manifested his awareness of the human factor in existence.

Challis, if he spoke little to Lewes of the Wonder during this time, maintained a strict observation of the child's doings.

The Wonder began his last volume of the Encyclopædia one Wednesday afternoon soon after lunch, and on Thursday morning, Challis was continually in and out of the room watching the child's progress, and noting his nearness to the end of the colossal task he had undertaken.

At a quarter to twelve he took up his old position in the doorway, and with his hands clasped behind his back he watched the reading of the last forty pages.

There was no slackening and no quickening in the Wonder's rate of progress. He read the articles under " Z " with the same attention he had given to the remainder of the work, and then, arrived at the last page, he closed the volume and took up the Index.

Challis suffered a qualm ; not so much on account of the possible postponement of the crisis he was awaiting, as because he saw that the reading of the Index could only be taken as a sign that the whole study had been unintelligent. No one could conceivably have any purpose in reading through an index.

And at this moment Lewes joined him in the doorway.

" What volume has he got to now ? " asked Lewes.

" The Index," returned Challis.

Lewes was no less quick in drawing his inference than Challis had been.

" Well, that settles it, I should think," was Lewes's comment.

" Wait, wait," returned Challis.

The Wonder turned a dozen pages at once, glanced at the new opening, made a further brief examination of two or three headings near the end of the volume, closed the book, and looked up.

" Have you finished ? " asked Challis.

The Wonder shook his head. " All this," he said—he indicated with a small and dirty hand the pile of volumes that were massed round him—" all this . . . " he repeated, hesitated for a word, and again shook his head with that solemn, deliberate impressiveness which marked all his actions.

Challis came towards the child, leaned over the table for a moment, and then sat down opposite to him. Between the two protagonists hovered Lewes, sceptical, inclined towards aggression.

" I am most interested," said Challis. " Will you try to tell me, my boy, what you think of—all this ? "

" So elementary . . . inchoate . . a disjunct-tive . . . patchwork," replied the Wonder. His abstracted eyes were blind to the objective world of our reality ; he seemed to be profoundly analysing the very elements of thought.

VII

Then that almost voiceless child found words. Heathcote's announcement of lunch was waved aside, the long afternoon waned, and still that thin trickle of sound flowed on.

The Wonder spoke in odd, pedantic phrases ; he used the technicalities of every science ; he constructed his sentences in unusual ways, and often he paused for a word and gave up the search, admitting that his meaning could not be expressed through the medium of any language known to him.

Occasionally Challis would interrupt him fiercely, would even rise from his chair and pace the room, arguing, stating a point of view, combating some suggestion that underlay the trend of that pitiless wisdom which in the end bore him down with its unanswerable insistence.

During those long hours much was stated by that small, thin voice which was utterly beyond the comprehension of the two listeners ; indeed, it is doubtful whether even Challis understood a tithe of the theory that was actually expressed in words.

As for Lewes, though he was at the time non-plussed, quelled, he was in the outcome impressed rather by the marvellous powers of memory exhibited than by the far finer powers shown in the super-human logic of the synthesis.

One sees that Lewes entered upon the interview with a mind predisposed to criticise, to destroy. There can be no doubt that as he listened his unin-formed mind was endeavouring to analyse, to weigh, and to oppose ; and this antagonism and his own thoughts continually interposed between him and the thought of the speaker. Lewes's account of what was spoken on that afternoon is utterly worthless.

Challis's failure to comprehend was not, at the outset, due to his antagonistic attitude. He began with an earnest wish to understand : he failed only because the thing spoken was beyond the scope of his intellectual powers. But he did, nevertheless, understand the trend of that analysis of progress ; he did in some half-realised way apprehend the gist of that terrible deduction of a final adjustment.

He must have apprehended, in part, for he fiercely combated the argument, only to quaver, at last, into a silence which permitted again that trickle of hesitating, pedantic speech, which was yet so over-whelming, so conclusive.

As the afternoon wore on, however, Challis's

attitude must have changed ; he must have assumed an armour of mental resistance not unlike the resistance of Lewes. Challis perceived, however dimly, that life would hold no further pleasure for him if he accepted that theory of origin, evolution, and final adjustment ; he found in this cosmogony no place for his own idealism ; and he feared to be convinced even by that fraction of the whole argument which he could understand.

We see that Challis, with all his apparent devotion to science, was never more than a dilettante. He had another stake in the world which, at the last analysis, he valued more highly than the acquisition of knowledge. Those means of ease, of comfort, of liberty, of opportunity to choose his work among various interests, were the ruling influence of his life. With it all Challis was an idealist, and unpractical. His genial charity, his refinement of mind, his unthinking generosity, indicate the bias of a character which inclined always towards a picturesque optimism. It is not difficult to understand that he dared not allow himself to be convinced by Victor Stott's appalling synthesis.

At last, when the twilight was deepening into night, the voice ceased, the child's story had been told, and it had not been understood. The Wonder never again spoke of his theory of life. He realised from that time that no one could comprehend him.

As he rose to go, he asked one question that, simple as was its expression, had a deep and wonderful significance.

" Is there none of my kind ? " he said.   " Is this," and he laid a hand on the pile of books before him, " is this all ? "

" There is none of your kind," replied Challis ; and the little figure born into a world that could not understand him, that was not ready to receive him, walked to the window and climbed out into the darkness.

.   .   .   .   .

(Henry Challis is the only man who could ever have given any account of that extraordinary analysis of life, and he made no effort to recall the fundamental basis of the argument, and so allowed his memory of the essential part to fade.   Moreover, he had a marked disinclination to speak of that afternoon or of anything that was said by Victor Stott during those six momentous hours of expression.   It is evident that Challis's attitude to Victor Stott was not unlike the attitude of Captain Wallis to Victor Stott's father on the occasion of Hampden-shire's historic match with Surrey.   " This man will have to be barred," Wallis said.   " It means the end of cricket."   Challis, in effect, thought that if Victor Stott were encouraged, it would mean the end of research, philosophy, all the mystery, idealism, and joy of life. Once, and once only, did Challis give me any idea of what he had learned during that afternoon's colloquy, and the substance of what Challis then told me will be found at the end of this volume.)

CHAPTER X

HIS PASTORS AND MASTERS

I

FOR many months after that long afternoon in the
library, Challis was affected with a fever of restless-
ness, and his work on the book stood still. He was
in Rome during May, and in June he was seized by
a sudden whim and went to China by the Trans-
Siberian railway. Lewes did not accompany him.
Challis preferred, one imagines, to have no intercourse with Lewes while the memory of certain pronouncements was still fresh. He might have been
tempted to discuss that interview, and if, as was
practically certain, Lewes attempted to pour contempt on the whole affair, Challis might have been
drawn into a defence which would have revived
many memories he wished to obliterate.

He came back to London in September—he made
the return journey by steamer—and found his
secretary still working at the monograph on the
primitive peoples of Melanesia.

Lewes had spent the whole summer in Challis's town house in Eaton Square, whither all the material had been removed two days after that momentous afternoon in the library of Challis Court.

" I have been wanting your help badly for some time, sir," Lewes said on the evening of Challis's return. " Are you proposing to take up the work again ? If not . . ." Gregory Lewes thought he was wasting valuable time.

" Yes, yes, of course ; I am ready to begin again now, if you care to go on with me," said Challis. He talked for a few minutes of the book without any great show of interest. Presently they came to a pause, and Lewes suggested that he should give some account of how his time had been spent.

" To-morrow," replied Challis, " to-morrow will be time enough. I shall settle down again in a few days." He hesitated a moment, and then said : " Any news from Chilborough ? "

" N-no, I don't think so," returned Lewes. He was occupied with his own interests ; he doubted Challis's intention to continue his work on the book— the announcement had been so half-hearted.

" What about that child ? " asked Challis.

" That child ? " Lewes appeared to have forgotten the existence of Victor Stott.

" That abnormal child of Stott's ? " prompted Challis.

"Oh! Of course, yes. I believe he still goes nearly every day to the library. I have been down there two or three times, and found him reading. He has learned the use of the index-catalogue. He can get any book he wants. He uses the steps."

"Do you know what he reads?"

"No; I can't say I do."

"What do you think will become of him?"

"Oh! these infant prodigies, you know," said Lewes with a large air of authority, "they all go the same way. Most of them die young, of course, the others develop into ordinary commonplace men rather under than over the normal ability. After all, it is what one would expect. Nature always maintains her average by some means or another. If a child like this with his abnormal memory were to go on developing, there would be no place for him in the world's economy. The idea is inconceivable."

"Quite, quite," murmured Challis, and after a short silence he added: "You think he will deteriorate, that his faculties will decay prematurely?"

"I should say there could be no doubt of it," replied Lewes.

"Ah! well. I'll go down and have a look at him, one day next week," said Challis; but he did not go till the middle of October.

The direct cause of his going was a letter from

12

Crashaw, who offered to come up to town, as the matter was one of " really peculiar urgency."

" I wonder if young Stott has been blaspheming again," Challis remarked to Lewes. " Wire the man that I'll go down and see him this afternoon. I shall motor. Say I'll be at Stoke about half-past three."

II

Challis was ushered into Crashaw's study on his arrival, and found the rector in company with another man—introduced as Mr. Forman—a jolly-looking, high-complexioned man of sixty or so, with a great quantity of white hair on his head and face ; he was wearing an old-fashioned morning-coat and grey trousers that were noticeably too short for him.

Crashaw lost no time in introducing the subject of " really peculiar urgency," but he rambled in his introduction.

" You have probably forgotten," he said, " that last spring I had to bring a most horrible charge against a child called Victor Stott, who has since been living, practically, as I may say, under your ægis, that is, he has, at least, spent a greater part of his day, er—playing in your library at Challis Court."

" Quite, quite ; I remember perfectly," said Challis. " I made myself responsible for him up to a certain point. I gave him an occupation. It was intended, was it not, to divert his mind from speaking against religion to the yokels?"

"Quite a character, if I may say so," put in Mr. Forman cheerfully.

Crashaw was seated at his study table; the affair had something the effect of an examining magistrate taking the evidence of witnesses.

"Yes, yes," he said testily; "I did ask your help, Mr. Challis, and I did, in a way, receive some assistance from you. That is, the child has to some extent been isolated by spending so much of his time at your house."

"Has he broken out again?" asked Challis.

"If I understand you to mean has the child been speaking openly on any subject connected with religion, I must say 'No,'" said Crashaw. "But he never attends any Sunday school, or place of worship; he has received no instruction in—er—any sacred subject, though I understand he is able to read; and his time is spent among books which, pardon me, would not, I suppose, be likely to give a serious turn to his thoughts."

"Serious?" questioned Challis.

"Perhaps I should say 'religious,'" replied Crashaw. "To me the two words are synonymous."

Mr. Forman bowed his head slightly with an air of

reverence, and nodded two or three times to express his perfect approval of the rector's sentiments.

" You think the child's mind is being perverted by his intercourse with the books in the library where he—he—' plays ' was your word, I believe ? "

" No, not altogether," replied Crashaw, drawing his eyebrows together. " We can hardly suppose that he is able at so tender an age to read, much less to understand, those works of philosophy and science which would produce an evil effect on his mind. I am willing to admit, since I, too, have had some training in scientific reading, that writers on those subjects are not easily understood even by the mature intelligence."

" Then why, exactly, do you wish me to prohibit the child from coming to Challis Court ? "

" Possibly you have not realised that the child is now five years old ? " said Crashaw with an air of conferring illumination.

" Indeed ! Yes. An age of some discretion, no doubt," returned Challis.

" An age at which the State requires that he should receive the elements of education," continued Crashaw.

" Eh ? " said Challis.

" Time he went to school," explained Mr. Forman. " I've been after him, you know. I'm the attendance officer for this district."

Challis for once committed a breach of good manners. The import of the thing suddenly appealed to his sense of humour : he began to chuckle and then he laughed out a great, hearty laugh, such as had not been stirred in him for twenty years.

" Oh ! forgive me, forgive me," he said, when he had recovered his self-control. " But you don't know ; you can't conceive the utter, childish absurdity of setting that child to recite the multiplication table with village infants of his own age. Oh ! believe me, if you could only guess, you would laugh with me. It's so funny, so inimitably funny."

" I fail to see, Mr. Challis," said Crashaw, " that there is anything in any way absurd or—or unusual in the proposition."

" Five is the age fixed by the State," said Mr. Forman. He had relaxed into a broad smile in sympathy with Challis's laugh, but he had now relapsed into a fair imitation of Crashaw's intense seriousness.

" Oh ! How can I explain ? " said Challis. " Let me take an instance. You propose to teach him, among other things, the elements of arithmetic ? "

" It is a part of the curriculum," replied Mr. Forman.

" I have only had one conversation with this child," went on Challis—and at the mention of that conversation his brows drew together and he became very grave again ; " but in the course of that conversation this child had occasion to refer, by way of illustration, to some abstruse theorem of the differential calculus. He did it, you will understand, by way of making his meaning clear—though the illustration was utterly beyond me : that reference represented an act of intellectual condescension."

" God bless me, you don't say so ? " said Mr. Forman.

" I cannot see," said Crashaw, " that this instance of yours, Mr. Challis, has any real bearing on the situation. If the child is a mathematical genius—there have been instances in history, such as Blaise Pascal—he would not, of course, receive elementary instruction in a subject with which he was already acquainted."

" You could not find any subject, believe me, Crashaw, in which he could be instructed by any teacher in a Council school."

" Forgive me, I don't agree with you," returned Crashaw. " He is sadly in need of some religious training."

" He would not get that at a Council school," said Challis, and Mr. Forman shook his head sadly, as though he greatly deprecated the fact.

" He must learn to recognise authority," said Crashaw. " When he has been taught the necessity of submitting himself to all his governors, teachers, spiritual pastors, and masters : ordering himself lowly and reverently to all his betters ; when, I say, he has learnt that lesson, he may be in a fit and proper condition to receive the teachings of the Holy Church."

Mr. Forman appeared to think he was attending divine service. If the rector had said " Let us pray," there can be no doubt that he would immediately have fallen on his knees.

Challis shook his head. " You can't understand, Crashaw," he said.

" I *do* understand," said Crashaw, rising to his feet, " and I intend to see that the statute is not disobeyed in the case of this child, Victor Stott."

Challis shrugged his shoulders ; Mr. Forman assumed an expression of stern determination.

" In any case, why drag me into it ? " asked Challis.

Crashaw sat down again. The flush which had warmed his sallow skin subsided as his passion died out. He had worked himself into a condition of righteous indignation, but the calm politeness of Challis rebuked him. If Crashaw prided himself on his devotion to the Church, he did not wish that attitude to overshadow the pride he also took in the belief that he was Challis's social equal. Crashaw's father had been a lawyer, with a fair practice in

Derby, but he had worked his way up to a partnership from the position of office-boy, and Percy Crashaw seldom forgot to be conscious that he was a gentleman by education and profession.

"I did not wish to *drag* you into this business," he said quietly, putting his elbows on the writing-table in front of him, and reassuming the judicial attitude he had adopted earlier; "but I regard this child as, in some sense, your protégé." Crashaw put the tips of his fingers together, and Mr. Forman watched him warily, waiting for his cue. If this was to be a case for prayer, Mr. Forman was ready, with a clean white handkerchief to kneel upon.

"In some sense, perhaps," returned Challis. "I haven't seen him for some months."

"Cannot you see the necessity of his attending school?" asked Crashaw, this time with an insinuating suavity; he believed that Challis was coming round.

"Oh!" Challis sighed with a note of expostulation. "Oh! the thing's grotesque, ridiculous."

"If that's so," put in Mr. Forman, who had been struck by a brilliant idea, "why not bring the child here, and let the Reverend Mr. Crashaw, or myself, put a few general questions to 'im?"

"Ye-es," hesitated Crashaw, "that might be done; but, of course, the decision does not rest with us."

"It rests with the Local Authority," mused Challis. He was running over three or four names of members of that body who were known to him.

"Certainly," said Crashaw, " the Local Education Authority alone has the right to prosecute, but——" He did not state his antithesis. They had come to the crux which Crashaw had wished to avoid. He had no weight with the committee of the L.E.A., and Challis's recommendation would have much weight. Crashaw intended that Victor Stott should attend school, but he had bungled his preliminaries : he had rested on his own authority, and forgotten that Challis had little respect for that influence. Conciliation was the only card to play now.

"If I brought him, he wouldn't answer your questions," sighed Challis. "He's very difficult to deal with."

"Is he, indeed?" sympathised Mr. Forman. "I've 'ardly seen 'im myself ; not to speak to, that is."

"He might come with his mother," suggested Crashaw.

Challis shook his head. "By the way, it is the mother whom you would proceed against?" he asked.

"The parent is responsible," said Mr. Forman. "She will be brought before a magistrate and fined for the first offence."

"I shan't fine her if she comes before me," replied Challis.

Crashaw smiled.   He meant to avoid that eventuality.

The little meeting lapsed into a brief silence. There seemed to be nothing more to say.

"Well," said Crashaw, at last, with a rising inflexion that had a conciliatory, encouraging, now-my-little-man kind of air, "We-ll, of course, no one wishes to proceed to extremes.   I think, Mr. Challis, I think I may say that you are the person who has most influence in this matter, and I cannot believe that you will go against the established authority both of the Church and the State.   If it were only for the sake of example."

Challis rose deliberately.   He shook his head, and unconsciously his hands went behind his back. There was hardly room for him to pace up and down, but he took two steps towards Mr. Forman, who immediately rose to his feet ; and then he turned and went over to the window.   It was from there that he pronounced his ultimatum.

"Regulations, laws, religious and lay authorities," he said, "come into existence in order to deal with the rule, the average.   That must be so.   But if we are a reasoning, intellectual people we must have some means of dealing with the exception.   That means rests with a consensus of intelligent opinion strong enough to set the rule upon one side.   In an overwhelming majority of cases there *is* no such con-

sensus of opinion, and the exceptional individual
suffers by coming within the rule of a law which
should not apply to him. Now, I put it to you, as
reasoning, intelligent men" ('ear, 'ear, murmured
Mr. Forman automatically), " are we, now that we
have the power to perform a common act of justice,
to exempt an unfortunate individual exception who
has come within the rule of a law that holds no application for him, or are we to exhibit a crass stupidity
by enforcing that law ? Is it not better to take the
case into our own hands, and act according to the
dictates of common sense ? "

" Very forcibly put," murmured Mr. Forman.

" I'm not finding any fault with the law or the
principle of the law," continued Challis ; " but it is,
it must be, framed for the average. We must use
our discretion in dealing with the exception—and
this is an exception such as has never occurred since
we have had an Education Act."

" I don't agree with you," said Crashaw, stubbornly. " I do not consider this an exception."

" But you *must* agree with me, Crashaw. I have
a certain amount of influence and I shall use it."

" In that case," replied Crashaw, rising to his
feet, " I shall fight you to the bitter end. I am
determined"—he raised his voice and struck the
writing-table with his fist—" I am *determined* that
this infidel child shall go to school. I am prepared,

if necessary, to spend all my leisure in seeing that the law is carried out."

Mr. Forman had also risen. "Very right, very right, indeed," he said, and he knitted his mild brows and stroked his patriarchal white beard with a simulation of stern determination.

"I think you would be better advised to let the matter rest," said Challis.

Mr. Forman looked inquiringly at the representative of the Church.

"I shall fight," replied Crashaw, stubbornly, fiercely.

"Ha!" said Mr. Forman.

"Very well, as you think best," was Challis's last word.

As Challis walked down to the gate, where his motor was awaiting him, Mr. Forman trotted up from behind and ranged himself alongside.

"More rain wanted yet for the roots, sir," he said. "September was a grand month for 'arvest, but we want rain badly now."

"Quite, quite," murmured Challis, politely. He shook hands with Mr. Forman before he got into the car.

Mr. Forman, standing politely bareheaded, saw that Mr. Challis's car went in the direction of Ailesworth.

CHAPTER XI

HIS EXAMINATION

I

CHALLIS'S first visit was paid to Sir Deane Elmer, that man of many activities, whose name inevitably suggests his favourite phrase of " Organised Progress "—with all its variants.

This is hardly the place in which to criticise a man of such diverse abilities as Deane Elmer, a man whose name still figures so prominently in the public press in connection with all that is most modern in eugenics ; with the Social Reform programme of the moderate party ; with the reconstruction of our penal system ; with education, and so many kindred interests ; and, finally, of course, with colour photography and process printing. This last Deane Elmer always spoke of as his hobby, but we may doubt whether all his interests were not hobbies in the same sense. He is the natural descendant of those earlier amateur scientists—the adjective conveys no reproach—of the nineteenth century, among whom we remember such striking figures as those of Lord Avebury and Sir Francis Galton.

In appearance Deane Elmer was a big, heavy, rather corpulent man, with a high complexion, and his clean-shaven jowl and his succession of chins hung in heavy folds. But any suggestion of material grossness was contradicted by the brightness of his rather pale-blue eyes, by his alertness of manner, and by his ready, whimsical humour.

As chairman of the Ailesworth County Council, and its most prominent unpaid public official—after the mayor—Sir Deane Elmer was certainly the most important member of the Local Authority, and Challis wisely sought him at once. He found him in the garden of his comparatively small establishment on the Quainton side of the town. Elmer was very much engaged in photographing flowers from nature through the ruled screen and colour filter—in experimenting with the Elmer process, in fact ; by which the intermediate stage of a coloured negative is rendered unnecessary. His apparatus was complicated and cumbrous.

" Show Mr. Challis out here," he commanded the man who brought the announcement.

" You must forgive me, Challis," said Elmer, when Challis appeared. " We haven't had such a still day for weeks. It's the wind upsets us in this process. Screens create a partial vacuum."

He was launched on a lecture upon his darling process before Challis could get in a word. It was best to let him have his head, and Challis took an intelligent interest.

It was not until the photographs were taken, and his two assistants could safely be trusted to complete the mechanical operations, that Elmer could be divorced from his hobby. He was full of jubilation. " We should have excellent results," he boomed— he had a tremendous voice—" but we shan't be able to judge until we get the blocks made. We do it all on the spot. I have a couple of platens in the shops here ; but we shan't be able to take a pull until to-morrow morning, I'm afraid. You shall have a proof, Challis. We *should* get magnificent results." He looked benignantly at the vault of heaven, which had been so obligingly free from any current of air.

Challis was beginning to fear that even now he would be allowed no opportunity to open the subject of his mission. But quite suddenly Elmer dropped the shutter on his preoccupation, and with that ready adaptability which was so characteristic of the man, forgot his hobby for the time being, and turned his whole attention to a new subject.

" Well ? " he said, " what is the latest news in anthropology ? "

"A very remarkable phenomenon," replied Challis. "That is what I have come to see you about."

"I thought you were in Paraguay pigging it with the Guaranis——"

"No, no; I don't touch the Americas," interposed Challis. "I want all your attention, Elmer. This is important."

"Come into my study," said Elmer, "and let us have the facts. What will you have—tea, whisky, beer?"

Challis's résumé of the facts need not be reported. When it was accomplished, Elmer put several keen questions, and finally delivered his verdict thus:

"We must see the boy, Challis. Personally I am, of course, satisfied, but we must not give Crashaw opportunity to raise endless questions, as he can and will. There is Mayor Purvis, the grocer, to be reckoned with, you must remember. He represents a powerful Nonconformist influence. Crashaw will get hold of him—and work him if we see Purvis first. Purvis always stiffens his neck against any breach of conventional procedure. If Crashaw saw him first, well and good, Purvis would immediately jump to the conclusion that Crashaw intended some subtle attack on the Nonconformist position, and would side with us."

"I don't think I know Purvis," mused Challis.

" Purvis & Co. in the Square," prompted Elmer.
" Black-and-white fellow; black moustache and
side whiskers, black eyes and white face. There's
a suggestion of the Methodist pulpit about him.
Doesn't appear in the shop much, and when he does,
always looks as if he'd sooner sell you a Bible than
a bottle of whisky."

" Ah, yes ! I know," said Challis. " I daresay
you're right, Elmer ; but it will be difficult to
persuade this child to answer any questions his
examiners may put to him."

" Surely he must be open to reason," roared
Elmer. " You tell me he has an extraordinary
intelligence, and in the next sentence you imply
that the child's a fool who can't open his mouth to
serve his own interests. What's your paradox ? "

" Sublimated material. Intellectual insight and
absolute spiritual blindness," replied Challis, getting
to his feet. " The child has gone too far in one
direction—in another he has made not one step. His
mind is a magnificent, terrible machine. He has
the imagination of a mathematician and a logician
developed beyond all conception, he has not one
spark of the imagination of a poet. And so he
cannot deal with men ; he can't understand their
weaknesses and limitations ; they are geese and hens
to him, creatures to be scared out of his vicinity.
However, I will see what I can do. Could you

13

arrange for the members of the Authority to come to my place ? ''

" I should think so. Yes," said Elmer. " I say, Challis, are you sure you're right about this child ? Sounds to me like some—some freak."

" You'll see," returned Challis. " I'll try and arrange an interview. I'll let you know."

" And, by the way," said Elmer, " you had better invite Crashaw to be present. He will put Purvis's back up, and that'll enlist the difficult grocer on our side probably."

When Challis had gone, Elmer stood for a few minutes, thoughtfully scratching the ample red surface of his wide, clean-shaven cheek. " I don't know," he ejaculated at last, addressing his empty study, " I don't know." And with that expression he put all thought of Victor Stott away from him, and sat down to write an exhaustive article on the necessity for a broader basis in primary education.

II

Challis called at the rectory of Stoke-Underhill on his way back to his own house.

" I give way," was the characteristic of his attitude to Crashaw, and the rector suppled his back again, remembered the Derby office-boy's tendency to brag, and made the amende honorable. He even overdid his magnanimity and came too near subservience—so lasting is the influence of the lessons of youth.

Crashaw did not mention that in the interval between the two interviews he had called upon Mr. Purvis in the Square. The ex-mayor had refused to commit himself to any course of action.

Challis forgot the rectory and all that it connoted before he was well outside the rectory's front door. Challis had a task before him that he regarded with the utmost distaste. He had warmly championed a cause ; he had been heated by the presentation of a manifest injustice which was none the less tyrannical because it was ridiculous. But now he realised that it was only the abstract question which had aroused his enthusiastic advocacy, and he shrank from the interview with Victor Stott—that small, deliberate, intimidating child.

Henry Challis, the savant, the man of repute in letters, the respected figure in the larger world ; Challis, the proprietor and landlord ; Challis, the power among known men, knew that he would have to plead, to humble himself, to be prepared for a rebuff—worst of all, to acknowledge the justice of taking so undignified a position. Any aristocrat may stoop with dignity when he condescends of his own free will ; but there are few who can submit gracefully to deserved contempt.

Challis was one of the few. He had many admirable qualities. Nevertheless, during that short motor ride from Stoke to his own house, he resented the indignity he anticipated, resented it intensely—and submitted.

III

He was allowed no respite. Victor Stott was emerging from the library window as Challis rolled up to the hall door. It was one of Ellen Mary's days—she stood respectfully in the background while her son descended ; she curtsied to Challis as he came forward.

He hesitated a moment. He would not risk insult in the presence of his chauffeur and Mrs. Stott. He confronted the Wonder ; he stood before him, and over him like a cliff.

" I must speak to you for a moment on a matter of some importance," said Challis to the little figure below him, and as he spoke he looked over the child's head at the child's mother. " It is a matter that concerns your own welfare. Will you come into the house with me for a few minutes ? "

Ellen Mary nodded, and Challis understood. He turned and led the way. At the door, however, he stood aside and spoke again to Mrs. Stott. " Won't you come in and have some tea, or something ? " he asked.

" No, sir, thank you, sir," replied Ellen Mary;
" I'll just wait 'ere till 'e's ready."

" At least come in and sit down," said Challis, and
she came in and sat in the hall. The Wonder had
already preceded them into the house. He had
walked into the morning-room—probably because
the door stood open, though he was now tall enough
to reach the handles of the Challis Court doors. He
stood in the middle of the room when Challis entered.

" Won't you sit down ? " said Challis.

The Wonder shook his head.

" I don't know if you are aware," began Challis,
" that there is a system of education in England at
the present time, which requires that every child
should attend school at the age of five years, unless
the parents are able to provide their children with
an education elsewhere."

The Wonder nodded.

Challis inferred that he need proffer no further
information with regard to the Education Act.

" Now, it is very absurd," he continued, " and I
have, myself, pointed out the absurdity ; but there
is a man of some influence in this neighbourhood
who insists that you should attend the elementary
school." He paused, but the Wonder gave no
sign.

" I have argued with this man," continued Challis,
" and I have also seen another member of the Local

Education Authority—a man of some note in the larger world—and it seems that you cannot be exempted unless you convince the Authority that your knowledge is such that to give you a Council school education would be the most absurd farce."

" Cannot you stand in loco parentis ? " asked the Wonder suddenly, in his still, thin voice.

" You mean," said Challis, startled by this outburst, " that I am in a sense providing you with an education ? Quite true; but there is Crashaw to deal with."

" Inform him," said the Wonder.

Challis sighed. " I have," he said, " but he can't understand." And then, feeling the urgent need to explain something of the motives that govern this little world of ours—the world into which this strangely logical exception had been born—Challis attempted an exposition.

" I know," he said, " that these things must seem to you utterly absurd, but you must try to realise that you are an exception to the world about you ; that Crashaw or I, or, indeed, the greatest minds of the present day, are not ruled by the fine logic which you are able to exercise. We are children compared to you. We are swayed even in the making of our laws by little primitive emotions and passions, self-interests, desires. And at the best we are not capable of ordering our lives and our government to those just ends which we may see, some of us, are abstractly right and fine. We are at the mercy of that great mass of the people who have not yet won to an intellectual and discriminating judgment of how their own needs may best be served, and whose representatives consider the interests of a party, a constituency, and especially of their own personal ambitions and welfare, before the needs of humanity as a whole, or even the humanity of these little islands.

"Above all, we are divided man against man. We are split into parties and factions, by greed and jealousies, petty spites and self-seeking, by unintelligence, by education, and by our inability—a mental inability—'to see life steadily and see it whole,' and lastly, perhaps chiefly, by our intense egotisms, both physical and intellectual.

"Try to realise this. It is necessary, because whatever your wisdom, you have to live in a world of comparative ignorance, a world which cannot appreciate you, but which can and will fall back upon the compelling power of the savage—the resort to physical, brute force."

The Wonder nodded. "You suggest—— ?" he said.

"Merely that you should consent to answer certain elementary questions which the members of the Local Authority will put to you," replied Challis.

" I can arrange that these questions be asked here—
in the library. Will you consent ? "

The Wonder nodded, and made his way into the
hall, without another word. His mother rose and
opened the front door for him.

As Challis watched the curious couple go down
the drive, he sighed again, perhaps with relief,
perhaps at the impotence of the world of men.

IV

There were four striking figures on the Education
Committee selected by the Ailesworth County
Council.

The first of these was Sir Deane Elmer, who was
also chairman of the Council at this time. The
second was the vice-chairman, Enoch Purvis, the ex-
mayor, commonly, if incorrectly, known as " Mayor "
Purvis.

The third was Richard Standing, J.P., who owned
much property on the Quainton side of the town.
He was a bluff, hearty man, devoted to sport and
agriculture ; a Conservative by birth and inclination,
a staunch upholder of the Church and the Tariff
Reform movement.

The fourth was the Rev. Philip Steven, a co-opted
member of the Committee, head master of the
Ailesworth Grammar School. Steven was a tall, thin

man with bent shoulders, and he had a long, thin face, the length of which was exaggerated by his square brown beard. He wore gold-mounted spectacles which, owing to his habit of dropping his head, always needed adjustment whenever he looked up. The movement of lifting his head and raising his hand to his glasses had become so closely associated, that his hand went up even when there was no apparent need for the action. Steven spoke of himself as a Broad Churchman, and in his speech on prize-day he never omitted some allusion to the necessity for "marching" or "keeping step" with the times. But Elmer was inclined to laugh at this assumption of modernity. "Steven," he said, on one occasion, "marks time and thinks he is keeping step. And every now and then he runs a little to catch up." The point of Elmer's satire lay in the fact that Steven was usually to be seen either walking very slowly, head down, lost in abstraction ; or—when aroused to a sense of present necessity—going with long strides as if intent on catching up with the times without further delay. Very often, too, he might be seen running across the school playground, his hand up to those elusive glasses of his. "There goes Mr. Steven, catching up with the times," had become an accepted phrase.

There were other members of the Education Committee, notably Mrs. Philip Steven, but they were subordinate. If those four striking figures were unanimous, no other member would have dreamed of expressing a contrary opinion. But up to this time they had not yet been agreed upon any important line of action.

This four, Challis and Crashaw met in the morning-room of Challis Court one Thursday afternoon in early June. Elmer had brought a stenographer with him for scientific purposes.

"Well," said Challis, when they were all assembled. "The—the subject—I mean, Victor Stott is in the library. Shall we adjourn?" Challis had not felt so nervous since the morning before he had sat for honours in the Cambridge Senate House.

In the library they found a small child, reading.

V

He did not look up when the procession entered, nor did he remove his cricket cap. He was in his usual place at the centre table.

Challis found chairs for the Committee, and the members ranged themselves round the opposite side of the table. Curiously, the effect produced was that of a class brought up for a viva voce examination, and when the Wonder raised his eyes and glanced deliberately down the line of his judges, this effect was heightened. There was an audible fidgeting, a creak of chairs, an indication of small embarrassments.

"Her—um!" Deane Elmer cleared his throat with noisy vigour; looked at the Wonder, met his eyes and looked hastily away again; "Hm!—her—rum!" he repeated, and then he turned to Challis. "So this little fellow has never been to school?" he said.

Challis frowned heavily. He looked exceedingly uncomfortable and unhappy. He was conscious that he could take neither side in this controversy—that he was in sympathy with no one of the seven other persons who were seated in his library.

He shook his head impatiently in answer to Sir Deane Elmer's question, and the chairman turned to the Rev. Philip Steven, who was gazing intently at the pattern of the carpet.

"I think, Steven," said Elmer, "that your large experience will probably prompt you to a more efficient examination than we could conduct. Will you initiate the inquiry?"

Steven raised his head slightly, put a readjusting hand up to his glasses, and then looked sternly at the Wonder over the top of them. Even the sixth form quailed when the head master assumed this expression, but the small child at the table was gazing out of the window.

Doubtless Steven was slightly embarrassed by the detachment of the examinee, and blundered. "What is the square root of 226 ? " he asked—he probably intended to say 225.

" 15·03329—to five places," replied the Wonder.

Steven started. Neither he nor any other member of the Committee was capable of checking that answer without resort to pencil and paper.

" Dear me ! " ejaculated Squire Standing.

Elmer scratched the superabundance of his purple jowl, and looked at Challis, who thrust his hands into his pockets and stared at the ceiling.

Crashaw leaned forward and clasped his hands together. He was biding his time.

" Mayor " Purvis alone seemed unmoved. " What's that book he's got open in front of him ? " he asked.

" May I see ? " interposed Challis hurriedly, and he rose from his chair, picked up the book in question, glanced at it for a moment, and then handed it to the grocer. The book was Van Vloten's Dutch text and Latin translation of Spinoza's Short Treatise.

The grocer turned to the title-page. " Ad—beany—dick—ti—de—Spy—nozer," he read aloud and then : " What's it all about, Mr. Challis ? " he asked. " German or something, I take it ? "

" In any case it has nothing to do with elementary

arithmetic," replied Challis curtly, " Mr. Steven will set your mind at ease on that point."

" Certainly, certainly," murmured Steven.

Grocer Purvis closed the book carefully and replaced it on the desk. " What does half a stone o' loaf sugar at two-three-farthings come to ? " he asked.

The Wonder shook his head. He did not understand the grocer's phraseology.

" What is seven times two and three quarters ? " translated Challis.

" 19·25," answered the Wonder.

" What's that in shillin's ? " asked Purvis.

" 1·60416."

" Wrong ! " returned the grocer triumphantly.

" Er—excuse me, Mr. Purvis," interposed Steven, " I think not. The—the—er—examinee has given the correct mathematical answer to five places of decimals—that is, so far as I can check him mentally."

" Well, it seems to me," persisted the grocer, " as he's gone a long way round to answer a simple question what any fifth-standard child could do in his head. I'll give him another."

" Cast it in another form," put in the chairman. " Give it as a multiplication sum."

Purvis tucked his fingers carefully into his waistcoat pockets. " I put the question, Mr. Chairman,"

he said, " as it'll be put to the youngster when he
has to tot up a bill. That seems to be a sound and
practical form for such questions to be put in."

Challis sighed impatiently. " I thought Mr.
Steven had been delegated to conduct the first part
of the examination," he said. " It seems to me that
we are wasting a lot of time."

Elmer nodded. " Will you go on, Mr. Steven ? "
he said.

Challis was ashamed for his compeers. " What
children we are," he thought.

Steven got to work again with various arithmetical
questions, which were answered instantly, and then
he made a sudden leap and asked : " What is the
binomial theorem ? "

" A formula for writing down the coefficient of
any stated term in the expansion of any stated power
of a given binomial," replied the Wonder.

Elmer blew out his cheeks and looked at Challis,
but met the gaze of Mr. Steven, who adjusted his
glasses and said, " I am satisfied under this
head."

" It's all beyond me," remarked Squire Standing
frankly.

" I think, Mr. Chairman, that we've had enough
theoretical arithmetic," said Purvis. " There's a
few practical questions I'd like to put."

" No more arithmetic, then," assented Elmer, and

Crashaw exchanged a glance of understanding with the grocer.

"Now, how old was our Lord when He began His ministry?" asked the grocer.

"Uncertain," replied the Wonder.

Mr. Purvis smiled. "Any Sunday-school child knows that!" he said.

"Of course, of course," murmured Crashaw.

But Steven looked uncomfortable. "Are you sure you understand the purport of the answer, Mr. Purvis?" he asked.

"Can there be any doubt about it?" replied the grocer. "I asked how old our Lord was when He began His ministry, and he"—he made an indicative gesture with one momentarily released hand towards the Wonder—"and he says he's 'uncertain.'"

"No, no," interposed Challis impatiently, "he meant that the answer to your question was uncertain."

"How's that?" returned the grocer. "I've always understood——"

"Quite, quite," interrupted Challis. "But what we have always understood does not always correspond to the actual fact."

"What did you intend by your answer?" put in Elmer quickly, addressing the Wonder.

"The evidence rests mainly on Luke's Gospel," answered the Wonder, "but the phrase '$\dot{\alpha}\rho\chi\acuteo\mu\epsilon\nu o\varsigma$

ὡσεὶ ἐτῶν τριάκοντα' is vague—it allows latitude in either direction. According to the chronology of John's Gospel the age might have been about thirty-two."

"It says 'thirty' in the Bible, and that's good enough for me," said the grocer, and Crashaw muttered "Heresy, heresy," in an audible under tone.

"Sounds very like blarsphemy to me," said Purvis, "like doubtin' the word of God. I'm for sending him to school."

Deane Elmer had been regarding the face of the small abstracted child with considerable interest. He put aside for the moment the grocer's intimation of his voting tendency.

"How many elements are known to chemists?" asked Elmer of the examinee.

"Eighty-one well characterised; others have been described," replied the Wonder.

"Which has the greatest atomic weight?" asked Elmer.

"Uranium."

"And that weight is?"

"On the oxygen basis of 16—238·5."

"Extraordinary powers of memory," muttered Elmer, and there was silence for a moment, a silence broken by Squire Standing, who, in a loud voice, asked suddenly and most irrelevantly, "What's your opinion of Tariff Reform?"

" An empirical question that cannot be decided from a theoretical basis," replied the Wonder.

Elmer laughed out, a great shouting guffaw. " Quite right, quite right," he said, his cheeks shaking with mirth. " What have you to say to that, Standing ? "

" I say that Tariff Reform's the only way to save the country," replied Squire Standing, looking very red and obstinate, " and if this Government——"

Challis rose to his feet. " Oh ! aren't you all satisfied ? " he said. " Is this Committee here to argue questions of present politics ? What more evidence do you need ? "

" I'm not satisfied," put in Purvis resolutely, " nor is the Rev. Mr. Crashaw, I fancy."

" He has no vote," said Challis. " Elmer, what do you say ? "

" I think we may safely say that the child has been, and is being, provided with an education elsewhere, and that he need not therefore attend the elementary school," replied Elmer, still chuckling.

" On a point of order, Mr. Chairman, is that what you put to the meeting ? " asked Purvis.

" This is quite informal," replied Elmer. " Unless we are all agreed, the question must be put to the full Committee."

" Shall we argue the point in the other room ? " suggested Challis.

14

"Certainly, certainly," said| Elmer. "We can return, if necessary."

And the four striking figures of the Education Committee filed out, followed by Crashaw and the stenographer.

Challis, coming last, paused at the door and looked back.

The Wonder had returned to his study of Spinoza.

Challis waved a hand to the unconscious figure. "I must join my fellow-children," he said grimly, "or they will be quarrelling."

VI

But when he joined his fellow-children, Challis stood at the window of the morning-room, attending little to the buzz of voices and the clatter of glasses which marked the relief from the restraint of the examination-room. Even the stenographer was talking; he had joined Crashaw and Purvis—a lemonade group; the other three were drinking whisky. The division, however, is arbitrary, and in no way significant.

Challis caught a fragment of the conversation here and there: a bull-roar from Elmer or Squire Standing; an occasional blatancy from Purvis; a vibrant protest from Crashaw; a hesitating tenor pronouncement from Steven.

" Extraordinary powers of memory. . . . It isn't facts, but what they stand for that I. . . . Don't know his Bible—that's good enough for me. . . . Heresy, heresy. . . . A phenomenal memory, of course, quite phenomenal, but——"

The simple exposition of each man's theme was dogmatically asserted, and through it all Challis, standing alone, hardly conscious of each individual utterance, was still conscious that the spirits of those six men were united in one thing, had they but known it. Each was endeavouring to circumscribe the powers of the child they had just left—each was insistent on some limitation he chose to regard as vital.

They came to no decision that afternoon. The question as to whether the Authority should prosecute or not had to be referred to the Committee.

At the last, Crashaw entered his protest and announced once more that he would fight the point to the bitter end.

Crashaw's religious hatred was not, perhaps, altogether free from a sense of affronted dignity, but it was nevertheless a force to be counted ; and he had that obstinacy of the bigot which has in the past contributed much fire and food to the pyre of martyrdom. He had, too, a power of initiative within certain limits. It is true that the bird on a free wing could avoid him with contemptuous ease, but along his own path he was a terrifying jugger-naut. Crashaw, thus circumscribed, was a power, a moving force.

But now he was seeking to crush, not some paralysed rabbit on the road, but an elusive spirit of swiftness which has no name, but may be figured as the genius of modernity. The thing he sought to obliterate ran ahead of him with a smiling facility and spat rearwards a vaporous jet of ridicule.

Crashaw might crush his clerical wideawake over his frowning eyebrows, arm himself with a slightly dilapidated umbrella, and seek with long, determined strides the members of the Local Education Authority, but far ahead of him had run an intelligence that represented the instructed common sense of modernity.

It was for Crashaw to realise—as he never could and never did realise—that he was no longer the dominant force of progress; that he had been out-stripped, left toiling and shouting vain words on a road that had served its purpose, and though it still remained and was used as a means of travel, was becoming year by year more antiquated and despised.

Crashaw toiled to the end, and no one knows how far his personal purpose and spite were satisfied, but he could never impede any more that elusive spirit of swiftness; it had run past him.

CHAPTER XII

MEANWHILE a child of five—all unconscious that he was being represented to various members of the Local Education Authority as a protégé under the especial care and tutelage of the greatest of local magnates—ran through a well-kept index of the books in the library of Challis Court—an index written clearly on cards that occupied a great nest of accessible drawers; two cards with a full description to each book, alphabetically arranged, one card under the title of the work and one under the author's name.

The child made no notes as he studied—he never wrote a single line in all his life; but when a drawer of that delightful index had been searched, he would walk here and there among the three rooms at his disposal, and by the aid of the flight of framed steps that ran smoothly on rubber-tyred wheels, he would take down now and again some book or another until, returning to the table at last to read, he sat in an enceinte of piled volumes that had been collected round him.

Sometimes he read a book from beginning to end, more often he glanced through it, turning a dozen pages at a time, and then pushed it on one side with a gesture displaying the contempt that was not shown by any change of expression.

On many afternoons the sombrely clad figure of a tall, gaunt woman would stand at the open casement of a window in the larger room, and keep a mystic vigil that sometimes lasted for hours. She kept her gaze fixed on that strange little figure whenever it roved up and down the suite of rooms or clambered the pyramid of brown steps that might have made such a glorious plaything for any other child. And even when her son was hidden behind the wall of volumes he had built, the woman would still stare in his direction, but then her eyes seemed to look inwards ; at such times she appeared to be wrapped in an introspective devotion.

Very rarely, the heavy-shouldered figure of a man would come to the doorway of the larger room, and also keep a silent vigil—a man who would stand for some minutes with thoughtful eyes and bent brows and then sigh, shake his head and move away, gently closing the door behind him.

There were few other interruptions to the silence of that chapel-like library. Half a dozen times in the first few months a fair-haired, rather supercilious young man came and fetched away a few volumes; but even he evidenced an inclination to walk on tip-toe, a tendency that mastered him whenever he forgot for a moment his self-imposed rôle of scorn. . . .

Outside, over the swelling undulations of rich grass the sheep came back with close-cropped, ungainly bodies to a land that was yellow with buttercups. But when one looked again, their wool hung about them, and they were snatching at short turf that was covered at the wood-side by a sprinkle of brown leaves. Then the sheep have gone, and the wood is black with February rain, and again the unfolding of the year is about us; a thickening of high twigs in the wood, a glint of green on the blackthorn. . . .

Nearly three cycles of death and birth have run their course, and then the strange little figure comes no more to the library at Challis Court.

PART III

MY ASSOCIATION
WITH THE WONDER

CHAPTER XIII

HCW I WENT TO PYM TO WRITE A BOOK

I

THE circumstance that had intrigued me for so long was determined with an abruptness only less remarkable than the surprise of the onset. Two deaths within six months brought to me, the first, a competence, the second, release from gall and bitterness. For the first time in my life I was a free man. At forty one can still look forward, and I put the past behind me and made plans for the future. There was that book of mine still waiting to be written.

It was wonderful how the detail of it all came back to me—the plan of it, the thread of development, even the very phrases that I had toyed with. The thought of the book brought back a train of associations. There was a phrase I had coined as I had walked out from Ailesworth to Stoke-Under-hill ; a chapter I had roughed out the day I went to see Ginger Stott at Pym. It seemed to me that the whole conception of the book was associated in some way with that neighbourhood. I remembered at last that I had first thought of writing it after my return from America, on the day that I had had that curious experience with the child in the train. It occurred to me that by a reversal of the process, I might regain many more of my original thoughts ; that by going to live, temporarily perhaps, in the neighbourhood of Ailesworth, I might revive other associations.

The picture of Pym presented itself to me very clearly. I remembered that I had once thought that Pym was a place to which I might retire one day in order to write the things I wished to write. I decided to make the dream a reality, and I wrote to Mrs. Berridge at the Wood Farm, asking her if she could let me have her rooms for the spring, summer, and autumn.

II

I was all aglow with excitement on the morning that I set out for the Hampden Hills. This was change, I thought, freedom, adventure. This was the beginning of life, my real entry into the joy of living.

The world was alight with the fire of growth. May had come with a clear sky and a torrent of green was flowing over field, hedge, and wood. I remember that I thanked " whatever gods there be," that one could live so richly in the enjoyment of these things.

III

Farmer Bates met me at Great Hittenden Station. His was the only available horse and cart at Pym, for the Berridges were in a very small way, and it is doubtful if they could have made both ends meet if Mrs. Berridge had not done so well by letting her two spare rooms.

I have a great admiration for Farmer Bates and Mrs. Berridge. I regret intensely that they should both have been unhappily married. If they had married each other they would undoubtedly have made a success of life.

Bates was a Cockney by birth, but always he had had an ambition to take a farm, and after twenty years of work as a skilled mechanic he had thrown up a well-paid job, and dared the uncertainties which beset the English farmer. That venture was a constant bone of strife between him and his wife. Mrs. Bates preferred the town. It has always seemed to me that there was something fine about Bates and his love for the land.

" Good growing weather, Mr. Bates," I said, as I climbed up into the cart.

"Shouldn't be sorry to see some more rain," replied Bates, and damped my ardour for a moment.

Just before we turned into the lane that leads up the long hill to Pym, we passed a ramshackle cart, piled up with a curious miscellany of ruinous furniture. A man was driving, and beside him sat a slatternly woman and a repulsive-looking boy of ten or twelve years old, with a great swollen head and an open, slobbering mouth.

I was startled. I jumped to the conclusion that this was the child I had seen in the train, the son of Ginger Stott.

As we slowed down to the ascent of the long hill, I said to Bates: "Is that Stott's boy?"

Bates looked at me curiously. "Why, no," he said. "Them's the 'Arrisons. 'Arrison's dead now; he was a wrong 'un, couldn't make a job of it, nohow. They used to live 'ere, five or six year ago, and now 'er 'usband's dead, Mrs. 'Arrison's coming back with the boy to live. Worse luck! We thought we was shut of 'em."

"Oh!" I said. "The boy's an idiot, I suppose."

"'Orrible," replied Bates, shaking his head, "'orrible; can't speak nor nothing; goes about bleating and baa-ing like an old sheep."

I looked round, but the ramshackle cart was

hidden by the turn of the road. "Does Stott still live at Pym?" I asked.

"Not Ginger," replied Bates. "He lives at Ailesworth. Mrs. Stott and 'er son lives here."

"The boy's still alive then?" I asked.

"Yes," said Bates.

"Intelligent child?" I asked.

"They say," replied Bates. "Book-learnin' and such. They say 'e's read every book in Mr. Challis's librairy."

"Does he go to school?"

"No. They let 'im off. Leastways Mr. Challis did. They say the Reverend Crashaw, down at Stoke, was fair put out about it."

I thought that Bates emphasised the "on dit" nature of his information rather markedly. "What do *you* think of him?" I asked.

"Me?" said Bates. "I don't worry my 'ead about him. I've got too much to *do*." And he went off into technicalities concerning the abundance of charlock on the arable land of Pym. He called it "garlic." I saw that it was typical of Bates that he should have too much to *do*. I reflected that his was the calling which begot civilisation.

IV

The best and surest route from Pym to the Wood Farm is, appropriately, by way of the wood; but in wet weather the alternative of various cart tracks that wind among the bracken and shrub of the Common, is preferable in many ways. May had been very dry that year, however, and Farmer Bates chose the wood. The leaves were still light on the beeches. I remember that as I tried to pierce the vista of stems that dipped over the steep fall of the hill, I promised myself many a romantic exploration of the unknown mysteries beyond.

Everything was so bright that afternoon that nothing, I believe, could have depressed me. When I looked round the low, dark room with its one window, a foot from the ground and two from the ceiling, I only thought that I should be out-of-doors all the time. It amused me that I could touch the ceiling with my head by standing on tiptoe, and I laughed at the framed " presentation plates " from old Christmas numbers on the walls. These things are merely curious when the sun is shining and it is high May, and one is free to do the desired work after twenty years in a galley.

v

At a quarter to eight that evening I saw the sun set behind the hills. As I wandered reflectively down the lane that goes towards Challis Court, a blackbird was singing ecstatically in a high elm; here and there a rabbit popped out and sat up, the

picture of precocious curiosity.   Nature seemed to
be standing in her doorway for a careless half-hour's
gossip, before putting up the shutters to bar the
robbers who would soon be about their work of the
night.

It was still quite light as I strolled back over the
Common, and I chose a path that took me through
a little spinney of ash, oak, and beech, treading carefully to avoid crushing the tender crosiers of bracken
that were just beginning to break their way through
the soil.

As I emerged from the little clump of wood, I saw
two figures going away from me in the direction of
Pym.

One was that of a boy wearing a cricket-cap ; he
was walking deliberately, his hands hanging at his
sides ; the other figure was a taller boy, and he
threw out his legs in a curious, undisciplined way,
as though he had little control over them.   At first
sight I thought he was not sober.

The two passed out of sight behind a clump of
hawthorn, but once I saw the smaller figure turn
and face the other, and once he made a repelling
gesture with his hands.

It occurred to me that the smaller boy was
trying to avoid his companion ; that he was, in
one sense, running away from him, that he walked
as one might walk away from some threatening

15

animal, deliberately—to simulate the appearance of courage.

I fancied the bigger boy was the idiot Harrison I had seen that afternoon, and Farmer Bates's "We hoped we were shut of him," recurred to me. I wondered if the idiot were dangerous or only a nuisance.

I took the smaller boy to be one of the villagers' children. I noticed that his cricket-cap had a dark patch as though it had been mended with some other material.

The impression which I received from this trivial affair was one of disappointment. The wood and the Common had been so deserted by humanity, so given up to nature, that I felt the presence of the idiot to be a most distasteful intrusion. "If that horrible thing is going to haunt the Common there will be no peace or decency," was the idea that presented itself. "I must send him off, the brute," was the rider. But I disliked the thought of being obliged to drive him away.

VI

The next morning I did not go on the Common ; I was anxious to avoid a meeting with the Harrison idiot. I had been debating whether I should drive him away if I met him. Obviously I had no more right on the Common than he had—on the other hand, he was a nuisance, and I did not see why I should allow him to spoil all my pleasure in that ideal stretch of wild land which pressed on three sides of the Wood Farm. It was a stupid quandary of my own making; but I am afraid it was rather typical of my mental attitude. I am prone to set myself tasks, such as this eviction of the idiot from common ground, and equally prone to avoid them by a process of procrastination.

By way of evasion I walked over to Deane Hill and surveyed the wonderful panorama of neat country that fills the basin between the Hampden and the Quainton Hills. Seen from that height, it has something the effect of a Dutch landscape, it all looks so amazingly tidy. Away to the left I looked over Stoke-Underhill. Ailesworth was a blur in the hollow, but I could distinguish the high fence of the County Ground.

I sat all the morning on Deane Hill, musing and smoking, thinking of such things as Ginger Stott, and the match with Surrey. I decided that I must certainly go and see Stott's queer son, the phenomenon who had, they say, read all the books in Mr. Challis's library. I wondered what sort of a library this Challis had, and who he was. I had never heard of him before. I think I must have gone to sleep for a time.

When Mrs. Berridge came to clear away my

dinner—I dined, without shame, at half-past twelve
—I detained her with conversation. Presently I
asked about little Stott.

" He's a queer one, that's what he is," said Mrs.
Berridge. She was a neat, comely little woman,
rather superior to her station, and it seemed to me,
certainly superior to her clod of a husband.

" A great reader, Farmer Bates tells me," I said.

Mrs. Berridge passed that by. " His mother's in
trouble about him this morning," she said. " She's
such a nice, respectable woman, and has all her milk
and eggs and butter off of us. She was here this
morning while you were out, sir, and, what I could
make of it that 'Arrison boy had been chasing her
boy on the Common last night."

" Oh ! " I said with sudden enlightenment. " I
believe I saw them." At the back of my mind I
was struggling desperately with a vague remembrance. It may sound incredible, but I had only
the dimmest memory of my later experience of the
child. The train incident was still fresh in my
mind, but I could not remember what Stott had told
me when I talked with him by the pond. I seemed to
have an impression that the child had some strange
power of keeping people at a distance; or was I
mixing up reality with some Scandinavian fairy tale?

" Very likely, sir," Mrs. Berridge went on.
" What upset Mrs. Stott was that her boy's never

upset by anything—he has a curious way of looking
at you, sir, that makes you wish you wasn't there;
but from what Mrs. Stott says, this 'Arrison boy
wasn't to be drove off, anyhow, and her son came in
quite flurried like. Mrs. Stott seemed quite put out
about it."

Doubtless I might have had more information
from my landlady, but I was struggling to reconstruct that old experience which had slipped away
from me, and I turned back to the book I had been
pretending to read. Mrs. Berridge was one of those
unusual women—for her station in life—who know
when to be silent, and she finished her clearing
away without initiating any further remarks.

When she had finished I went out on to the Common and looked for the pond where I had talked
with Ginger Stott.

I found it after a time, and then I began to gather
up the threads I had dropped.

It all came back to me, little by little. I remembered that talk I had had with him, his very gestures;
I remembered how he had spoken of habits, or the
necessity for the lack of them, and that took me
back to the scene in the British Museum Reading-
Room, and to my theory. I was suddenly alive to
that old interest again.

I got up and walked eagerly in the direction of
Mrs. Stott's cottage.

CHAPTER XIV

THE INCIPIENCE OF MY SUBJECTION TO THE WONDER

I

VICTOR STOTT was in his eighth year when I met him for the third time. I must have stayed longer than I imagined by the pond on the Common, for Mrs. Stott and her son had had tea, and the boy was preparing to go out. He stopped when he saw me coming ; an unprecedented mark of recognition, so I have since learned.

As I saw him then, he made a remarkable, but not a repulsively abnormal figure. His baldness struck one immediately, but it did not give him a look of age. Then one noticed that his head was unmistakably out of proportion to his body, yet the disproportion was not nearly so marked as it had been in infancy. These two things were conspicuous ; the less salient peculiarities were observed later ; the curious little beaky nose that jutted out at an unusual angle from the face, the lips that were too straight and determined for a child, the laxity of the limbs when the body was in repose—lastly, the eyes.

When I met Victor Stott on this, third, occasion, there can be no doubt that he had lost something of his original power. This may have been due to his long sojourn in the world of books, a sojourn that had, perhaps, altered the strange individuality of his thought ; or it may have been due, in part at least, to his recent recognition of the fact that the power of his gaze exercised no influence over creatures such as the Harrison idiot. Nevertheless, though something of the original force had abated, he still had an extraordinary, and, so far as I can learn, altogether unprecedented power of enforcing his will without word or gesture ; and I may say here that in those rare moments when Victor Stott looked me in the face, I seemed to see a rare and wonderful personality peering out through his eyes. That was the personality which had, no doubt, spoken to Challis and Lewes through that long afternoon in the library of Challis Court. Normally one saw a curious, unattractive, rather repulsive figure of a child ; when he looked at one with that rare look of intention, the man that lived within that unattractive body was revealed, his insight, his profundity, his unexampled wisdom. If we mark the difference between man and animals by a measure of intelligence, then surely this child was a very god among men.

II

Victor Stott did not look at me when I entered his mother's cottage; I saw only the unattractive exterior of him, and I blundered into an air of patronage.

" Is this your boy ? " I said, when I had greeted her. " I hear he is a great scholar."

" Yes, sir," replied Ellen Mary quietly. She never boasted to strangers.

" You don't remember me, I suppose ? " I went on, foolishly ; trying, however, to speak as to an equal. " You were in petticoats the last time I saw you."

The Wonder was standing by the window, his arms hanging loosely at his sides ; he looked out aslant up the lane ; his profile was turned towards me. He made no answer to my question.

" Oh yes, sir, he remembers," replied Ellen Mary. " He never forgets anything."

I paused, uncomfortably. I was slightly huffed by the boy's silence.

" I have come to spend the summer here," I said at last. " I hope he will come to see me. I have brought a good many books with me; perhaps he might care to read some of them."

I had to talk *at* the boy ; there was no alternative. Inwardly I was thinking that I had Kant's Critique and Hegel's Phenomenology among my books. " He may put on airs of scholarship," I thought ; " but I fancy that he will find those two works rather above the level of his comprehension as yet." I did not recognise the fact that it was I who was putting on airs, not Victor Stott.

" 'E's given up reading the past six weeks, sir," said Ellen Mary, " but I daresay he will come and see your books."

She spoke demurely, and she did not look at her son ; I received the impression that her statements were laid before him to take up, reject, or pass unnoticed as he pleased.

I was slightly exasperated. I turned to the Wonder. " Would you care to come ? " I asked.

He nodded without looking at me, and walked out of the cottage.

I hesitated.

" 'E'll go with you now, sir," prompted Ellen Mary. " That's what 'e means."

I followed the Wonder in a condition of suppressed irritation. " His mother might be able to interpret his rudeness," I thought, " but I would teach him to convey his intentions more clearly. The child had been spoilt."

III

The Wonder chose the road over the Common. I should have gone by the wood, but when we came to the entrance of the wood, he turned up on to the Common. He did not ask me which way I preferred. Indeed, we neither of us spoke during the half-mile walk that separated the Wood Farm from the last cottage in Pym.

I was fuming inwardly. I had it in my mind at that time to put the Wonder through some sort of an examination. I was making plans to contribute towards his education, to send him to Oxford, later. I had adumbrated a scheme to arouse interest in his case among certain scholars and men of influence with whom I was slightly acquainted. I had been very much engrossed with these plans as I had made my way to the Stotts' cottage. I was still somewhat exalted in mind with my dreams of a vicarious brilliance. I had pictured the Wonder's magnificent passage though the University ; I had acted, in thought, as the generous and kindly benefactor. . . . It had been a grandiose dream, and the reality was so humiliating. Could I make this mannerless child understand his possibilities ? Had he any ambition ?

Thinking of these things, I had lagged behind as we crossed the Common, and when I came to the gate of the farmyard, the Wonder was at the door of the house. He did not wait for me, but walked straight into my sitting-room. When I entered, I found him seated on the low window-sill, turning over the top layer of books in the large case which had been opened, but not unpacked. There was no place to put the books ; in fact, I was proposing to have some shelves put up, if Mrs. Berridge had no objection.

I entered the room in a condition of warm indignation. "Cheek" was the word that was in my mind. "Confounded cheek," I muttered. Nevertheless I did not interrupt the boy ; instead, I lit a cigarette, sat down and watched him.

I was sceptical at first. I noted at once the sure touch with which the boy handled my books, the practised hand that turned the pages, the quick examination of title-page and the list of contents, the occasional swift reference to the index, but I did not believe it possible that any one could read so fast as he read when he did condescend for a few moments to give his attention to a few consecutive pages. "Was it a pose ?" I thought, yet he was certainly an adept in handling the books. I was puzzled, yet I was still sceptical—the habit of experience was towards disbelief—a boy of seven and a half could not possibly have the mental equipment to skim all that philosophy. . . .

My books were being unpacked very quickly. Kant, Hegel, Schelling, Fichte, Leibnitz, Nietzsche, Hume, Bradley, William James had all been rejected and were piled on the floor, but he had hesitated longer over Bergson's *Creative Evolution*. He really seemed to be giving that some attention, though he read it—if he were reading it—so fast that the hand which turned the pages hardly rested between each movement.

When Bergson was sent to join his predecessors, I determined that I would get some word out of this strange child—I had never yet heard him speak, not a single syllable. I determined to brave all rebuffs. I was prepared for that.

"Well?" I said, when Bergson was laid down. "Well! What do you make of that?"

He turned and looked out of the window.

I came and sat on the end of the table within a few feet of him. From that position I, too, could see out of the window, and I saw the figure of the Harrison idiot slouching over the farmyard gate.

A gust of impatience whirled over me. I caught up my stick and went out quickly.

"Now then," I said, as I came within speaking distance of the idiot, "get away from here. Out with you!"

The idiot probably understood no word of what I said, but like a dog he was quick to interpret my tone and gesture. He made a revoltingly inhuman sound as he shambled away, a kind of throaty yelp. I walked back to the house. I could not avoid the feeling that I had been unnecessarily brutal.

When I returned the Wonder was still staring out of the window ; but though I did not guess it then, the idiot had served my purpose better than my determination. It was to the idiot that I owed my subsequent knowledge of Victor Stott. The Wonder had found a use for me. He was resigned to bear with my feeble mental development, because I was strong enough to keep at bay that half-animal creature who appeared to believe that Victor Stott was one of his own kind—the only one he had ever met. The idiot in some unimaginable way had inferred a likeness between himself and the Wonder— they both had enormous heads—and the idiot was the only human being over whom the Wonder was never able to exercise the least authority.

IV

I went in and sat down again on the end of the table. I was rather heated. I lit another cigarette and stared at the Wonder, who was still looking out of the window.

There was silence for a few seconds, and then he spoke of his own initiative.

" Illustrates the weakness of argument from history and analogy," he said in a clear, small voice, addressing no one in particular. " Hegel's limitations are qualitatively those of Harrison, who argues that I and he are similar in kind."

The proposition was so astounding that I could find no answer immediately. If the statement had been made in boyish language I should have laughed at it, but the phraseology impressed me.

" You've read Hegel, then ? " I asked evasively.

" Subtract the endeavour to demonstrate a pre-conceived hypothesis from any known philosophy," continued the Wonder, without heeding my question, " and the remainder, the only valuable material, is found to be distorted." He paused as if waiting for my reply.

How could one answer such propositions as these offhand ? I tried, however, to get at the gist of the sentence, and, as the silence continued, I said with some hesitation : " But it is impossible, surely, to approach the work of writing, say a philosophy, without some apprehension of the end in view ? "

" Illogical," replied the Wonder, " not philo-sophy ; a system of trial and error—to evaluate a complex variable function." He paused a moment, and then glanced down at the pile of books on the floor. " More millions," he said.

I think he meant that more millions of books

might be written on this system without arriving at
an answer to the problem, but I admit that I am
at a loss, that I cannot interpret his remarks.   I
wrote them down within an hour or two after they
were uttered, but I may have made mistakes.   The
mathematical metaphor is beyond me.   I have no
acquaintance with higher mathematics.

The Wonder had a very expressionless face, but I
thought at this moment that he wore a look of
sadness ; and that look was one of the factors which
helped me to understand the unbridgeable gulf that
lay between his intellect and mine.   I think it was
at this moment that I first began to change my
opinion.   I had been regarding him as an unbearable
little prig, but it flashed across me as I watched him
now, that his mind and my own might be so far
differentiated that he was unable to convey his
thoughts to me.   " Was it possible," I wondered,
" that he had been trying to talk down to my level ?"

" I am afraid I don't quite follow you," I said.
I had intended to question him further, to urge him
to explain, but it came to me that it would be quite
hopeless to go on.   How can one answer the unreasoning questions of a child ?   Here I was the
child, though a child of slightly advanced development.   I could appreciate that it was useless to
persist in a futile " Why, why ? " when the answer
could only be given in terms that I could not com-

prehend. Therefore I hesitated, sighed, and then with that obstinacy of vanity which creates an image of self-perfection and refuses to relinquish it, I said :

" I wish you could explain yourself ; not on this particular point of philosophy, but your life——" I stopped, because I did not know how to phrase my demand. What was it, after all, that I wanted to learn ?

" That I can't explain," said the Wonder. " There are no data."

I saw that he had accepted my request for explanation in a much wider sense than I had intended, and I took him up on this.

" But haven't you any hypothesis ? "

" I cannot work on the system of trial and error," replied the Wonder.

Our conversation went no further this afternoon, for Mrs. Berridge came in to lay the cloth. She looked askance, I thought, at the figure on the window-sill, but she ventured no remark save to ask if I was ready for my supper.

" Yes, oh ! yes ! " I said.

" Shall I lay for two, sir ? " asked Mrs. Berridge.

" Will you stay and have supper ? " I said to the Wonder, but he shook his head, got up and walked out of the room. I watched him cross the farmyard and make his way over the Common.

" Well ! " I said to Mrs. Berridge, when the boy

was out of sight, "that child is what in America they call ' the limit,' Mrs. Berridge."

My landlady put her lips together, shook her head, and shivered slightly. " He gives me the shudders," she said.

V

I neither read nor wrote that evening. I forgot to go out for a walk at sunset. I sat and pondered until it was time for bed, and then I pondered myself to sleep. No vision came to me, and I had no relevant dreams.

The next morning at seven o'clock I saw Mrs. Stott come over the Common to fetch her milk from the farm. I waited until her business was done, and then I went out and walked back with her.

" I want to understand about your son," I said by way of making an opening.

She looked at me quickly. " You know, 'e 'ardly ever speaks to me, sir," she said.

I was staggered for a moment. " But you understand him ? " I said.

" In some ways, sir," was her answer.

I recognised the direction of the limitation. " Ah ! we none of us understand him in all ways," I said, with a touch of patronage.

" No, sir," replied Ellen Mary. She evidently agreed to that statement without qualification.

16

"But what is he going to do?" I asked. "When he grows up, I mean?"

"I can't say, sir. We must leave that to 'im."

I accepted the rebuke more mildly than I should have done on the previous day. "He never speaks of his future?" I said feebly.

"No, sir."

There seemed to be nothing more to say. We had only gone a couple of hundred yards, but I paused in my walk. I thought I might as well go back and get my breakfast. But Mrs. Stott looked at me as though she had something more to say. We stood facing each other on the cart track.

"I suppose I can't be of any use?" I asked vaguely.

Ellen Mary broke suddenly into volubility.

"I 'ope I'm not askin' too much, sir," she said, "but there is a way you could 'elp if you would. 'E 'ardly ever speaks to me, as I've said, but I've been opset about that 'Arrison boy. 'E's a brute beast, sir, if you know what I mean, and *'e* (she differentiated her pronouns only by accent, and where there is any doubt I have used italics to indicate that her son is referred to) "doesn't seem to 'ave the same 'old on 'im as *'e* does over others. It's truth, I am not easy in my mind about it, sir, although *'e* 'as never said a word to me, not being afraid of anything like other children, but 'e seems to have took a sort of a fancy to you, sir " (I think this was intended as the subtlest flattery), "and if you was to go with 'im when 'e takes 'is walks—'e's much in the air, sir, and a great one for walkin'—I think 'e'd be glad of your cump'ny, though maybe 'e won't never say it in so many words. You mustn't mind 'im being silent, sir; there's some things we can't understand, and though, as I say, 'e 'asn't said anything to me, it's not that I'm scheming be'ind 'is back, for I know 'is meaning without words being necessary."

She might have said more, but I interrupted her at this point. " Certainly, I will come and fetch him,"—I lapsed unconsciously into her system of denomination—" this morning, if you are sure he would like to come out with me."

" I'm quite sure, sir," she said.

" About nine o'clock ? " I asked.

" That would do nicely, sir," she answered.

As I walked back to the farm I was thinking of the life of those two occupants of the Stotts' cottage. The mother who watched her son in silence, studying his every look and action in order to gather his meaning ; who never asked her son a question nor expected from him any statement of opinion ; and the son wrapped always in that profound speculation which seemed to be his only mood. What a household !

It struck me while I was having breakfast that I seemed to have let myself in for a duty that might prove anything but pleasant.

VI

There is nothing to say of that first walk of mine with the Wonder. I spoke to him once or twice and he answered by nodding his head; even this notice I now know to have been a special mark of favour, a condescension to acknowledge his use for me as a guardian. He did not speak at all on this occasion.

I did not call for him in the afternoon; I had made other plans. I wanted to see the man Challis, whose library had been at the disposal of this phenomenal child. Challis might be able to give me further information. The truth of the matter is that I was in two minds as to whether I would stay at Pym through the summer, as I had originally intended. I was not in love with the prospect which the sojourn now held out for me. If I were to be constituted head nursemaid to Master Victor Stott, there would remain insufficient time for the progress of my own book on certain aspects of the growth of the philosophic method.

I see now, when I look back, that I was not convinced at that time, that I still doubted the Wonder's

learning. I may have classed it as a freakish pedan-
try, the result of a phenomenal memory.

Mrs. Berridge had much information to impart
on the subject of Henry Challis. He was her husband's landlord, of course, and his was a hallowed
name, to be spoken with decency and respect. I am
afraid I shocked Mrs. Berridge at the outset by my
casual " Who's this man Challis ? " She certainly
atoned by her own manner for my irreverence ; she
very obviously tried to impress me. I professed
submission, but was not intimidated, rather my
curiosity was aroused.

Mrs. Berridge was not able to tell me the one thing
I most desired to know, whether the lord of Challis
Court was in residence ; but it was not far to walk,
and I set out about two o'clock.

VII

Challis was getting into his motor as I walked up
the drive. I hurried forward to catch him before
the machine was started. He saw me coming and
paused on the doorstep.

" Did you want to see me ? " he asked, as I came
up.

" Mr. Challis ? " I asked.

" Yes," he said.

" I won't keep you now," I said, " but perhaps

you could let me know some time when I could see
you."

"Oh, yes," he said, with the air of a man who is
constantly subjected to annoyance by strangers.
"But perhaps you wouldn't mind telling me what
it is you wish to see me about? I might be able to
settle it now, at once."

"I am staying at the Wood Farm," I began. "I
am interested in a very remarkable child——"

"Ah! take my advice, leave him alone," interrupted Challis quickly.

I suppose I looked my amazement, for Challis
laughed. "Oh, well," he said, "of course you
won't take such spontaneous advice as that.
I'm in no hurry. Come in." He took off his
heavy overcoat and threw it into the tonneau.
"Come round again in an hour," he said to the
chauffeur.

"It's very good of you," I protested, "I could
come quite well at any other time."

"I'm in no hurry," he repeated. "You had better
come to the scene of Victor Stott's operations. He
hasn't been here for six weeks, by the way. Can
you throw any light on his absence?"

I made a friend that afternoon. When the car
came back at four o'clock, Challis sent it away
again. "I shall probably stay down here to-
night," he said to the butler, and to me: "Can

you stay to dinner ? I must convince you about this child."

" I have dined once to-day," I said. " At half-past twelve. I have no other excuse."

" Oh ! well," said Challis, " you needn't eat, but I must. Get us something, Heathcote," he said to the butler, " and bring tea here."

Much of our conversation after dinner was not relevant to the subject of the Wonder ; we drifted into a long argument upon human origins which has no place here. But by that time I had been very well informed as to all the essential facts of the Wonder's childhood, of his entry into the world of books, of his earlier methods, and of the significance of that long speech in the library. But at that point Challis became reserved. He would give me no details.

" You must forgive me ; I can't go into that," he said.

" But it is so incomparably important," I protested.

" That may be, but you must not question me. The truth of the matter is that I have a very confused memory of what the boy said, and the little I might remember, I prefer to leave undisturbed."

He piqued my curiosity, but I did not press him. It was so evident that he did not wish to speak on that head.

He walked up with me to the farm at ten o'clock and came into my room.

"We need not keep you out of bed, Mrs. Berridge," he said to my flustered landlady. "I daresay we shall be up till all hours. We promise to see that the house is locked up." Mr. Berridge stood a figure of subservience in the background.

My books were still heaped on the floor. Challis sat down on the window-sill and looked over some of them. "Many of these Master Stott probably read in my library," he remarked, "in German. Language is no bar to him. He learns a language as you or I would learn a page of history."

Later on, I remember that we came down to essentials. "I must try and understand something of this child's capacities," I said in answer to a hint of Challis's that I should leave the Wonder alone. "It seems to me that here we have something which is of the first importance, of greater importance, indeed, than anything else in the history of the world."

"But you can't make him speak," said Challis.

"I shall try," I said. "I recognise that we cannot compel him, but I have a certain hold over him. I see from what you have told me that he has treated me with most unusual courtesy. I assure you that several times when I spoke to him this morning he nodded his head."

" A good beginning," laughed Challis.

" I can't understand," I went on, " how it is that you are not more interested. It seems to me that this child knows many things which we have been patiently attempting to discover since the dawn of civilisation."

" Quite," said Challis. " I admit that, but . . . well, I don't think I want to know."

" Surely," I said, " this key to all knowledge——"

" We are not ready for it," replied Challis. " You can't teach metaphysics to children."

Nevertheless my ardour was increased, not abated, by my long talk with Challis.

" I shall go on," I said, as I went out to the farm gate with him at half-past two in the morning.

" Ah ! well," he answered, " I shall come over and see you when I come back." He had told me earlier that he was going abroad for some months.

We hesitated a moment by the gate, and instinctively we both looked up at the vault of the sky and the glimmering dust of stars.

The same thought was probably in both our minds, the thought of the insignificance of this little system that revolves round one of the lesser lights of the Milky Way, but that thought was not to be expressed save by some banality, and we did not speak.

" I shall certainly look you up when I come back,"
said Challis.

" Yes ; I hope you will," I said lamely.

I watched the loom of his figure against the vague
background till I could distinguish it no longer.

CHAPTER XV

THE PROGRESS AND RELAXATION OF MY SUBJECTION

I

THE memory of last summer is presented to me now as a series of pictures, some brilliant, others vague, others again so uncertain that I cannot be sure how far they are true memories of actual occurrences, and how far they are interwoven with my thoughts and dreams. I have, for instance, a recollection of standing on Deane Hill and looking down over the wide panorama of rural England, through a driving mist of fine rain. This might well be counted among true memories, were it not for the fact that clearly associated with the picture is an image of myself grown to enormous dimensions, a Brocken spectre that threatened the world with titanic gestures of denouncement, and I seem to remember that this figure was saying : " All life runs through my fingers like a handful of dry sand." And yet the remembrance has not the quality of a dream.

I was, undoubtedly, overwrought at times. There were days when the sight of a book filled me with physical nausea, with contempt for the littleness, the narrow outlook, that seemed to me to characterise every written work. I was fiercely, but quite impotently, eager at such times to demonstrate the futility of all the philosophy ranged on the rough wooden shelves in my gloomy sitting-room. I would walk up and down and gesticulate, struggling, fighting to make clear to myself what a true philosophy should set forth. I felt at such times that all the knowledge I needed for so stupendous a task was present with me in some inexplicable way, was even pressing upon me, but that my brain was so clogged and heavy that not one idea of all that priceless wisdom could be expressed in clear thought. "I have never been taught to think," I would complain, "I have never perfected the machinery of thought," and then some dictum thrown out haphazard by the Wonder—his conception of light conversation—would recur to me, and I would realise that however well I had been trained, my limitations would remain, that I was an undeveloped animal, only one stage higher than a totem-fearing savage, a creature of small possibilities, incapable of dealing with great problems.

Once the Wonder said to me, in a rare moment of lucid condescension to my feeble intellect, " You figure space as a void in three dimensions, and time as a line that runs across it, and all other conceptions you relegate to that measure." He implied that this was a cumbrous machinery which had no relation to reality, and could define nothing. He told me that his idea of force, for example, was a pure abstraction, for which there was no figure in my mental outfit.

Such pronouncements as these left me struggling like a drowning man in deep water. I felt that it *must* be possible for me to come to the surface, but I could do nothing but flounder ; beat fiercely with limbs that were so powerful and yet so utterly useless. I saw that my very metaphors symbolised my feebleness ; I had no terms for my own mental condition ; I was forced to resort to some inapplicable physical analogy.

These fits of revolt against the limitations of human thought grew more frequent as the summer progressed. Day after day my self-sufficiency and conceit were being crushed out of me. I was always in the society of a boy of seven whom I was forced to regard as immeasurably my intellectual superior. There was no department of useful knowledge in which I could compete with him. Compete indeed ! I might as well speak of a third-standard child competing with Macaulay in a general knowledge paper.

" *Useful* knowledge," I have written, but the phrase needs definition. I might have taught the Wonder many things, no doubt ; the habits of men in great cities, the aspects of foreign countries, or the subtleties of cricket ; but when I was with him I felt—and my feelings must have been typical— that such things as these were of no account.

Towards the end of the summer, the occasions upon which I was able to stimulate myself into a condition of bearable complacency were very rare. I often thought of Challis's advice to leave the Wonder alone. I should have gone away if I had been free, but Victor Stott had a use for me, and I was powerless to disobey him. I feared him, but he controlled me at his will. I feared him as I had once feared an imaginary God, but I did not hate him.

One curious little fragment of wisdom came to me as the result of my experience—a useless fragment perhaps, but something that has in one way altered my opinion of my fellow-men. I have learnt that a measure of self-pride, of complacency, is essential to every human being. I judge no man any more for displaying an overweening vanity, rather do I envy him this representative mark of his humanity. The Wonder was completely and quite inimitably devoid of any conceit, and the word ambition had no meaning for him. It was inconceivable that he should compare himself with any of his fellow-creatures, and it was inconceivable that any honour they might have lavished upon him would have given him one moment's pleasure. He was entirely alone among aliens who were unable to comprehend him, aliens who could not flatter him, whose opinions were valueless to him. He had no more common ground on which to air his knowledge, no more grounds for comparison by which to achieve self-conceit than a man might have in a world tenanted only by sheep. From what I have heard him say on the subject of our slavery to preconceptions, I think the metaphor of sheep is one which he might have approved.

But the result of all this, so far as I am concerned, is a feeling of admiration for those men who are capable of such magnificent approval for themselves, the causes they espouse, their family, their country, and their species ; it is an approval which I fear I can never again attain in full measure.

I have seen possibilities which have enforced a humbleness that is not good for my happiness or conducive to my development. Henceforward I will espouse the cause of vanity. It is only the vain who deprecate vanity in others.

But there were times in the early period of my association with Victor Stott when I rebelled vigorously against his complacent assumption of my ignorance.

II

May was a gloriously fine month, and we were much out of doors. Unfortunately, except for one fortnight in August, that was all the settled weather we had that summer.

I remember sitting one afternoon staring at the same pond that Ginger Stott had stared at when he told me that the boy now beside me was a " blarsted freak."

The Wonder had said nothing that day, but now he began to enunciate some of his incomprehensible commonplaces in that thin, clear voice of his. I wrote down what I could remember of his utterances when I went home, but now I read them over again I am exceedingly doubtful whether I reported him correctly. There is, however, one dictum which seems clearly phrased, and when I recall the scene, I remember trying to push the induction he had started. The pronouncement, as I have it written, is as follows :

" Pure deduction from a single premiss, unaided by previous knowledge of the functions of the terms used in the expansion of the argument, is an act of creation, incontrovertible, and outside the scope of human reasoning."

I believe he meant to say—but my notes are horribly confused—that logic and philosophy were only relative, being dependent always in a greater or less degree upon the test of a material experiment for verification.

Here, as always, I find the Wonder's pronouncements very elusive. In one sense I see that what I have quoted here is a self-evident proposition, but I have the feeling that behind it there lies some gleam of wisdom which throws a faint light on the profound problem of existence.

I remember that in my own feeble way I tried to analyse this statement, and for a time I thought I had grasped one significant aspect of it. It seemed to me that the possibility of conceiving a philosophy that was not dependent for verification upon material experiment—that is to say, upon evidence afforded by the five senses—indicates that there is something which is not matter ; but that since the development of such a philosophy is not possible to our minds, we must argue that our dependence upon matter is so intimate that it is almost impossible to conceive that we are actuated by any impulse which does not arise out of a material complex.

At the back of my mind there seemed to be a thought that I could not focus, I trembled on the verge of some great revelation that never came.

Through my thoughts there ran a thread of reverence for the intelligence that had started my speculations. If only he could speak in terms that I could understand.

I looked round at the Wonder. He was, as usual, apparently lost in abstraction, and quite unconscious of my regard.

The wind was strong on the Common, and he sniffed once or twice and then wiped his nose. He did not use a handkerchief.

It came to me at the moment that he was no more than a vulgar little village boy.

III

There were few incidents to mark the progress of that summer. I marked the course of time by my own thoughts and feelings, especially by my growing submission to the control of the Wonder.

It was curious to recall that I had once thought of correcting the Wonder's manners, of administering, perhaps, a smacking. That was a fault of ignorance. I had often erred in the same way in other experiences of life, but I had not taken the lesson to heart. I remember at school our " head " taking us—I was in the lower fifth then—in Latin verse. He rebuked me for a false quantity, and I, very cocksure, disputed the point and read my line. The head pointed out very gravely that I had been misled by an English analogy in my pronunciation of the word " maritus," and I grew very hot and ashamed and apologetic. I feel much the same now when I think of my early attitude towards the Wonder. But this time, I think, I have profited by my experience.

There is, however, one incident which in the light of subsequent events it seems worth while to record.

One afternoon in early July, when the sky had lifted sufficiently for us to attempt some sort of a walk, we made our way down through the sodden woods in the direction of Deane Hill.

As we were emerging into the lane at the foot of the slope, I saw the Harrison idiot lurking behind the trunk of a big beech. This was only the third time I had seen him since I drove him away from the farm, and on the two previous occasions he had not come close to us.

This time he had screwed up his courage to follow us. As we climbed the lane I saw him slouching up the hedge-side behind us.

The Wonder took no notice, and we continued our way in silence.

When we reached the prospect at the end of the hill, where the ground falls away like a cliff and you have a bird's-eye view of two counties, we sat down on the steps of the monument erected in honour of those Hampdenshire men whose lives were thrown away in the South-African war.

That view always has a soothing effect upon me, and I gave myself up to an ecstasy of contemplation and forgot, for a few moments, the presence of the Wonder, and the fact that the idiot had followed us.

I was recalled to existence by the sound of a foolish, conciliatory mumbling, and looked round to see the leering face of the Harrison idiot ogling the Wonder from the corner of the plinth. The Wonder was between me and the idiot, but he was apparently oblivious of either of us.

I was about to rise and drive the idiot away, but the Wonder, still staring out at some distant horizon, said quietly, " Let him be."

I was astonished, but I sat still and awaited events.

The idiot behaved much as I have seen a very young and nervous puppy behave.

He came within a few feet of us, gurgling and crooning, flapping his hands and waggling his great head ; his uneasy eyes wandered from the Wonder to me and back again, but it was plainly the Wonder whom he wished to propitiate. Then he suddenly backed as if he had dared too much, flopped on to the wet grass and regarded us both with foolish, goggling eyes. For a few seconds he lay still, and then he began to squirm along the ground towards us, a few inches at a time, stopping every now and again to bleat and gurgle with that curious, crooning note which he appeared to think would pacificate the object of his overtures.

I stood by, as it were, ready to obey the first hint that the presence of this horrible creature was distasteful to the Wonder, but he gave no sign.

The idiot had come within five or six feet of us, wriggling himself along the wet grass, before the Wonder looked at him. The look when it came was one of those deliberate, intentional stares which made one feel so contemptible and insignificant.

The idiot evidently regarded this look as a sign of encouragement. He knelt up, began to flap his hands and changed his crooning note to a pleased, emphatic bleat.

"A-ba-ba," he blattered, and made uncouth gestures, by which I think he meant to signify that he wanted the Wonder to come and play with him.

Still the Wonder gave no sign, but his gaze never wavered, and though the idiot was plainly not intimidated, he never met that gaze for more than a second or two. Nevertheless he came on, walking now on his knees, and at last stretched out a hand to touch the boy he so curiously desired for a playmate.

That broke the spell. The Wonder drew back quickly—he never allowed one to touch him—got up and climbed two or three steps higher up the

base of the monument. "Send him away," he said
to me.

"That'll do," I said threateningly to the idiot,
and at the sound of my voice and the gesture of my
hand, he blenched, yelped, rolled over away from
me, and then got to his feet and shambled off for
several yards before stopping to regard us once more
with his pacificatory, disgusting ogle.

"Send him away," repeated the Wonder, as I
hesitated, and I rose to my feet and pretended to
pick up a stone.

That was enough. The idiot yelped again and
made off. This time he did not stop, though he
looked over his shoulder several times as he lolloped
away among the low gorse, to which look I replied
always with the threat of an imaginary stone.

The Wonder made no comment on the incident as
we walked home. He had shown no sign of fear.
It occurred to me that my guardianship of him was
merely a convenience, not a protection from any
danger.

IV

As time went on it became increasingly clear to
me that my chance of obtaining the Wonder's
confidence was becoming more and more remote.

At first he had replied to my questions; usually,
it is true, by no more than an inclination of his head.

but he soon ceased to make even this acknowledgment of my presence.

So I fell by degrees into a persistent habit of silence, admitted my submission by obtruding neither remark nor question upon my constant companion, and gave up my intention of using the Wonder as a means to gratify my curiosity concerning the problem of existence.

Once or twice I saw Crashaw at a distance. He undoubtedly recognised the Wonder, and I think he would have liked to come up and rebuke him— perhaps me, also; but probably he lacked the courage. He would hover within sight of us for a few minutes, scowling, and then stalk away. He gave me the impression of being a dangerous man, a thwarted fanatic, brooding over his defeat. If I had been Mrs. Stott, I should have feared the intrusion of Crashaw more than the foolish overtures of the Harrison idiot. But there was, of course, the Wonder's compelling power to be reckoned with, in the case of Crashaw.

V

Challis came back in early September, and it was he who first coaxed, and then goaded me into rebellion.

Challis did not come too soon.

At the end of August I was seeing visions, not pleasant, inspiriting visions, but the indefinite, perplexing shapes of delirium.

I think it must have been in August that I stood on Deane Hill, through an afternoon of fine, driving rain, and had a vision of myself playing tricks with the sands of life.

I had begun to lose my hold on reality. Silence, contemplation, a long-continued wrestle with the profound problems of life, were combining to break up the intimacy of life and matter, and my brain was not of the calibre to endure the strain.

Challis saw at once what ailed me.

He came up to the farm one morning at twelve o'clock. The date was, I believe, the twelfth of September. It was a brooding, heavy morning, with half a gale of wind blowing from the south-west, but it had not rained, and I was out with the Wonder when Challis arrived.

He waited for me and talked to the flattered Mrs. Berridge, remonstrated kindly with her husband for his neglect of the farm, and incidentally gave him a rebate on the rent.

When I came in, he insisted that I should come to lunch with him at Challis Court.

I consented, but stipulated that I must be back at Pym by three o'clock to accompany the Wonder for his afternoon walk.

Challis looked at me curiously, but allowed the stipulation.

We hardly spoke as we walked down the hill—the habit of silence had grown upon me, but after lunch Challis spoke out his mind.

On that occasion I hardly listened to him, but he came up to the farm again after tea and marched me off to dinner at the Court. I was strangely plastic when commanded, but when he suggested that I should give up my walks with the Wonder, go away. . . . I smiled and said " Impossible," as though that ended the matter.

Challis, however, persisted, and I suppose I was not too far gone to listen to him. I remember his saying : " That problem is not for you or me or any man living to solve by introspection. Our work is to add knowledge little by little, data here and there, for future evidence."

The phrase struck me, because the Wonder had once said " There are no data," when in the early days I had asked him whether he could say definitely if there was any future existence possible for us ?

Now Challis put it to me that our work was to find data, that every little item of real knowledge added to the feeble store man has accumulated in his few thousand years of life, was a step, the greatest step any man could possibly make.

" But could we not get, not a small but a very important item, from Victor Stott ? "

Challis shook his head. " He is too many thousands of years ahead of us," he said. " We can only bridge the gap by many centuries of patient toil. If a revelation were made to us, we should not understand it."

So, by degrees, Challis's influence took possession of me and roused me to self-assertion.

One morning, half in dread, I stayed at home and read a novel—no other reading could hold my attention—philosophy had become nauseating.

I expected to see the strange little figure of the Wonder come across the Common, but he never came, nor did I receive any reproach from Ellen Mary. I think she had forgotten her fear of the Harrison idiot.

Nevertheless, I did not give up my guardianship all at once. Three times after that morning I took the Wonder for a walk. He made no allusion to my defalcations. Indeed he never spoke. He relinquished me as he had taken me up, without comment or any expression of feeling.

VI

On the twenty-ninth of September I went down to Challis Court and stayed there for a week. Then I returned for a few days to Wood Farm in order to put my things together and pack my books. I had decided to go to Cairo for the winter with Challis.

At half-past one o'clock on Thursday, the eighth of October, I was in the sitting-room, when I saw the figure of Mrs. Stott coming across the Common. She came with a little stumbling run. I could see that she was agitated even before she reached the farmyard gate.

CHAPTER XVI

RELEASE

I

She opened the front door without knocking, and came straight into my sitting-room.

" 'E's not 'ere," she said in a manner that left it doubtful whether she made an assertion or asked a question.

" Your son ? " I said.   I had risen when she came into the room, " No ; I haven't seen him to-day."

Ellen Mary was staring at me, but it was clear that she neither saw nor heard me.   She had a look of intense concentration.   One could see that she was calculating, thinking, thinking.   . . .

I went over to her and took her by the arm.   I gently shook her.   " Now, tell me what's the matter ?   What has happened ? " I asked.

She made an effort to collect herself, loosened her arm from my hold and with an instinctive movement pushed forward the old bonnet, which had slipped to the back of her head.

"''E 'asn't been in to 'is dinner," she said hurriedly. "I've been on the Common looking for 'im."

"He may have made a mistake in the time," I suggested.

She made a movement as though to push me on one side, and turned towards the door. She was calculating again. Her expresion said quite plainly, "Could he be there, could he be *there*?"

"Come, come," I said, "there is surely no need to be anxious yet."

She turned on me. "''E never makes a mistake in the time," she said fiercely, "'e always knows the time to the minute without clock or watch. Why did you leave 'im alone?"

She broke off in her attack upon me and continued: "''E's never been late before, not a minute, and now it's a hour after 'is time."

"He may be at home by now," I said. She took the hint instantly and started back again with the same stumbling little run.

I picked up my hat and followed her.

II

The Wonder was not at the cottage.

"Now, my dear woman, you must keep calm," I said. "There is absolutely no reason to be disturbed. You had better go to Challis Court and see if he is in the library, I——"

" I'm a fool," broke in Ellen Mary with sudden decision, and she set off again without another word. I followed her back to the Common and watched her out of sight. I was more disturbed about her than about the non-appearance of the Wonder. He was well able to take care of himself, but she . . . . How strange that with all her calculations she had not thought of going to Challis Court, to the place where her son had spent so many days. I began to question whether the whole affair was not, in some way, a mysterious creation of her own disordered brain.

Nevertheless, I took upon myself to carry out that part of the programme which I had not been allowed to state in words to Mrs. Stott, and set out for Deane Hill. It was just possible that the Wonder might have slipped down that steep incline and injured himself. Possible, but very unlikely ; the Wonder did not take the risks common to boys of his age, he did not disport himself on dangerous slopes.

As I walked I felt a sense of lightness, of relief from depression. I had not been this way by myself since the end of August. It was good to be alone and free.

The day was fine and not cold, though the sun was

hidden. I noticed that the woods showed scarcely a mark of autumn decline.

There was not a soul to be seen by the monument. I scrambled down the slope and investigated the base of the hill and came back another way through the woods. I saw no one. I stopped continually and whistled loudly. If he is anywhere near at hand, I thought, and in trouble, he will hear that and answer me. I did not call him by name. I did not know what name to call. It would have seemed absurd to have called " Victor." No one ever addressed him by name.

My return route brought me back to the south edge of the Common, the point most remote from the farm. There I met a labourer whom I knew by sight, a man named Hawke. He was carrying a stick, and prodding with it foolishly among the furze and gorse bushes. The bracken was already dying down.

" What are you looking for ? " I asked.

" It's this 'ere Master Stott, sir," he said, looking up. " 'E's got loarst seemingly."

I felt a sudden stab of self-reproach. I had been taking things too easily. I looked at my watch. It was a quarter to four.

" Mr. Challis 'ave told me to look for 'un," added the man, and continued his aimless prodding of the gorse.

" Where is Mr. Challis ? " I asked.

" 'E's yonder, soomewheres." He made a vague gesture in the direction of Pym.

The sun had come out, and the Common was all aglow. I hastened towards the village.

On the way I met Farmer Bates and two or three labourers. They, too, were beating among the gorse and brown bracken. They told me that Mr. Challis was at the cottage and I hurried on. All the neighbourhood, it seems, were searching for the Wonder. In the village I saw three or four women standing with aprons over their heads, talking together.

I had never seen Pym so animated.

III

I met Challis in the lane. He was coming away from Mrs. Stott's cottage.

" Have you found him ? " I asked stupidly. I knew quite well that the Wonder was not found, and yet I had a fond hope that I might, nevertheless, be mistaken.

Challis shook his head. " There will be a mad woman in that cottage if he doesn't come back by nightfall," he remarked with a jerk of his head. " I've done what I can for her."

I explained that I had been over to Deane Hill, searching and calling.

" You didn't see anything ? " asked Challis,
echoing my foolish query of a moment before. I
shook my head.

We were both agitated without doubt.

We soon came up with Farmer Bates and his men.
They stopped and touched their hats when they
saw us, and we put the same silly question to them.

" You haven't found him ? " We knew perfectly
well that they would have announced the fact at
once if they had found him.

" One of you go over to the Court and get any
man you can find to come and help," said Challis.
" Tell Heathcote to send every one."

One of the labourers touched his cap again, and
started off at once with a lumbering trot.

Challis and I walked on in silence, looking keenly
about us and stopping every now and then and
calling. We called " Hallo ! Hallo-o ! " It was
an improvement upon my whistle.

" He's such a little chap," muttered Challis once ;
" it would be so easy to miss him if he were unconscious."

It struck me that the reference to the Wonder
was hardly sufficiently respectful. I had never
thought of him as " a little chap." But Challis had
not known him so intimately as I had.

The shadows were fast creeping over the Common.
At the woodside it was already twilight. The whole

18

of the western sky right up to the zenith was a finely shaded study in brilliant orange and yellow. "More rain," I thought instinctively, and paused for a moment to watch the sunset. The black distance stood clearly silhouetted against the sky. One could discern the sharp outline of tiny trees on the distant horizon.

We met Heathcote and several other men in the lane.

"Shan't be able to do much to-night, sir," said Heathcote. "It'll be dark in 'alf an hour, sir."

"Well, do what you can in half an hour," replied Challis, and to me he said, "You'd better come back with me. We've done what we can."

I had a picture of him then as the magnate; I had hardly thought of him in that light before. The arduous work of the search he could delegate to his inferiors. Still, he had come out himself, and I doubt not that he had been altogether charming to the bewildered, distraught mother.

I acquiesced in his suggestion. I was beginning to feel very tired.

Mrs. Heathcote was at the gate when we arrived at the Court. "'Ave they found 'im, sir?" she asked.

"Not yet," replied Challis.

I followed him into the house.

IV

As I walked back at ten o'clock it was raining steadily. I had refused the offer of a trap. I went through the dark and sodden wood, and I lingered and listened. The persistent tap, tap, tap of the rain on the leaves irritated me. How could one hear while that noise was going on ? There was no other sound. There was not a breath of wind. Only that perpetual tap, tap, tap, patter, patter, drip, tap, tap. It seemed as if it might go on through eternity. . . .

I went to the Stotts' cottage, though I knew there could be no news. Challis had given strict instructions that any news should be brought to him immediately. If it was bad news it was to be brought to him before the mother was told.

There was a light burning in the cottage, and the door was set wide open.

I went up to the door but I did not go in.

Ellen Mary was sitting in a high chair, her hands clasped together, and she rocked continually to and fro. She made no sound ; she merely rocked herself with a steady, regular persistence.

She did not see me standing at the open door, and I moved quietly away.

As I walked over the Common—I avoided the wood deliberately—I wondered what was the human limit of endurance. I wondered whether Ellen Mary had not reached that limit.

Mrs. Berridge had not gone to bed, and there were some visitors in the kitchen. I heard them talking. Mrs. Berridge came out when I opened the front door.

" Any news, sir ? " she asked.

" No ; no news," I said. I had been about to ask her the same question.

v

I did not go to sleep for some time. I had a picture of Ellen Mary before my eyes, and I could still hear that steady pat, patter, drip, of the rain on the beech leaves.

In the night I awoke suddenly, and thought I heard a long, wailing cry out on the Common. I got up and looked out of the window, but I could see nothing. The rain was still falling, but there was a blur of light that showed where the moon was shining behind the clouds. The cry, if there had been a cry, was not repeated.

I went back to bed and soon fell asleep again.

I do not know whether I had been dreaming, but I woke suddenly with a presentation of the little pond on the Common very clear before me.

" We never looked in the pond," I thought, and then—" but he could not have fallen into the pond ; besides, it's not two feet deep."

It was full daylight, and I got up and found that it was nearly seven o'clock.

The rain had stopped, but there was a scurry of low, threatening cloud that blew up from the south.

I dressed at once and went out. I made my way directly to the Stotts' cottage.

The lamp was still burning and the door open, but Ellen Mary had fallen forward on to the table ; her head was pillowed on her arms.

" There *is* a limit to our endurance," I reflected, " and she has reached it."

I left her undisturbed.

Outside I met two of Farmer Bates's labourers going back to work.

" I want you to come up with me to the pond," I said.

VI

The pond was very full.

On the side from which we approached, the ground sloped gradually, and the water was stretching out far beyond its accustomed limits.

On the farther side the gorse among the trunks of

the three ash-trees came right to the edge of the bank. On that side the bank was three or four feet high.

We came to the edge of the pond, and one of the labourers waded in a little way—the water was very shallow on that side—but we could see nothing for the scum of weed, little spangles of dirty green, and a mass of some other plant that had borne a little white flower in the earlier part of the year—stuff like dwarf hemlock.

Under the farther bank, however, I saw one comparatively clear space of black water.

" Let's go round," I said, and led the way.

There was a tiny path which twisted between the gorse roots and came out at the edge of the farther bank by the stem of the tallest ash. I had seen tiny village boys pretending to fish from this point with a stick and a piece of string. There was a dead branch of ash some five or six feet long, with the twigs partly twisted off ; it was lying among the bushes. I remembered that I had seen small boys using this branch to clear away the surface weed. I picked it up and took it with me.

I wound one arm round the trunk of the ash, and peered over into the water under the bank.

I caught sight of something white under the water. I could not see distinctly. I thought it was a piece of broken ware—the bottom of a basin.

I had picked up the ash stick and was going to probe the deeper water with it. Then I saw that the dim white object was globular.

The end of my stick was actually in the water. I withdrew it quickly, and threw it behind me.

My heart began to throb painfully.

I turned my face away and leaned against the ash-tree.

" Can you see anythin' ? " asked one of the labourers who had come up behind me.

" Oh ! Christ ! " I said. I turned quickly from the pond and pressed a way through the gorse.

I was overwhelmingly and disgustingly sick.

VII

By degrees the solid earth ceased to wave and sway be foreme like a rolling heave of water, and I looked up, pressing my hands to my head—my hands were as cold as death.

My clothes were wet and muddy where I had lain on the sodden ground. I got to my feet and instinctively began to brush at the mud.

I was still a little giddy, and I swayed and sought for support.

I could see the back of one labourer. He was kneeling by the ash-tree bending right down over the water. The other man was standing in the pond, up to his waist in water and mud.   I could just see his head and shoulders. . . .

I staggered away in the direction of the village.

VIII

I found Ellen Mary still sitting in the same chair. The lamp was fluttering to extinction, the flame leaping spasmodically, dying down till it seemed that it had gone out, and then again suddenly flickering up with little clicking bursts of flame. The air reeked intolerably of paraffin.

I blew the lamp out and pushed it on one side.

There was no need to break the news to Ellen Mary.   She had known last night, and now she was beyond the reach of information.

She sat upright in her chair and stared out into the immensity.   Her hands alone moved, and they were not still for an instant.   They lay in her lap, and her fingers writhed and picked at her dress.

I spoke to her once, but I knew that her mind was beyond the reach of my words.

" It is just as well," I thought ; " but we must get her away."

I went out and called to the woman next door.

She was in her kitchen, but the door was open. She came out when I knocked.

" Poor thing," she said, when I told her.   " It 'as

been a shock, no doubt. She was so wrapped hup in the boy."

She could hardly have said less if her neighbour had lost half-a-crown.

"Get her into your cottage before they come," I said harshly, and left her.

I wanted to get out of the lane before the men came back, but I had hardly started before I saw them coming.

They had made a chair of their arms, and were carrying him between them. They had not the least fear of him, now.

IX

The Harrison idiot suddenly jumped out of the hedge.

I put my hand to my throat. I wanted to cry out, to stop him, but I could not move. I felt sick again, and utterly weak and powerless, and I could not take my gaze from that little doll with the great drooping head that rolled as the men walked.

I was reminded, disgustingly, of children with a guy.

The idiot ran shambling down the lane. He knew the two men, who tolerated him and laughed at him. He was not afraid of them nor their burden.

He came right up to them. I heard one of the men say gruffly, " Now then, you cut along off ! "

I believe the idiot must have touched the dead body.

I was gripping my throat in my hand; I was trying desperately to cry out.

Whether the idiot actually touched the body or not I cannot say, but he must have realised in his poor, bemused brain that the thing was dead.

He cried out with his horrible, inhuman cry, turned, and ran up the lane towards me. He fell on his face a few yards from me, scrambled wildly to his feet again and came on yelping and shrieking. He was wildly, horribly afraid. I caught sight of his face as he passed me, and his mouth was distorted into a square, his upper lip horribly drawn up over his ragged, yellow teeth. Suddenly he dashed at the hedge and clawed his way through. I heard him still yelping appallingly as he rushed away across the field. . . .

CHAPTER XVII

IMPLICATIONS

I

THE jury returned a verdict of " Accidental death."

If there had been any traces of a struggle, I had not noticed them when I came to the edge of the pond. There may have been marks as if a foot had slipped. I was not thinking of evidence when I looked into the water.

There were marks enough when the police came to investigate, but they were the marks made by a twelve-stone man in hobnail boots, who had scrambled into, and out of, the pond. As the inspector said, it was not worth while wasting any time in looking for earlier traces of footsteps below those marks.

Nor were there any signs of violence on the body. It was in no way disfigured, save by the action of the water, in which it had lain for eighteen hours.

There was, indeed, only one point of any significance from the jury's point of view, and that they put on one side, if they considered it at all; the body was pressed into the mud.

The Coroner asked a few questions about this fact.

Was the mud very soft? Yes, very soft, liquid on top.

How was the body lying? Face downwards.

What part of the body was deepest in the mud? The chest. The witness said he had hard work to get the upper part of the body released; the head was free, but the mud held the rest. "The mooad soocked like," was the expressive phrase of the witness.

The Coroner passed on to other things. Had any one a spite against the child? and such futilities. Only once more did he revert to that solitary significant fact. "Would it be possible," he asked of the abashed and self-conscious labourer, "would it be possible for the body to have worked its way down into the soft mud as you have described it to have been found?"

"We-el," said the witness, "'twas in the stacky mooad, 'twas through the sarft stoof."

"But this soft mud would suck any solid body down, would it not?" persisted the Coroner.

And the witness recalled the case of a duck that had been sucked into the same soft pond mud the summer before, and cited the instance. He forgot to add that on that occasion the mud had not been under water.

The Coroner accepted the instance. There can be no question that both he and the jury were anxious to accept the easier explanation.

II

But I know perfectly well that the Wonder did not fall into the pond by accident.

I should have known, even if that conclusive evidence with regard to his being pushed into the mud had never come to light.

He may have stood by the ash-tree and looked into the water, but he would never have fallen. He was too perfectly controlled; and, with all his apparent abstraction, no one was ever more alive to the detail of his surroundings. He and I have walked together perforce in many slippery places, but I have never known him to fall or even begin to lose his balance, whereas I have gone down many times.

Yes; I know that he was pushed into the pond, and I know that he was held down in the mud, most probably by the aid of that ash stick I had held. But it was not for me to throw suspicion on any one at that inquest, and I preferred to keep my thoughts and my inferences to myself. I should have done so, even if I had been in possession of stronger evidence.

I hope that it was the Harrison idiot who was to blame. He was not dangerous in the ordinary sense, but he might quite well have done the thing in play —as he understood it. Only I cannot quite understand his pushing the body down after it fell. That seems to argue vindictiveness—and a logic which I can hardly attribute to the idiot. Still, who can tell what went on in the distorted mind of that poor creature ? He is reported to have rescued the dead body of a rabbit from the undergrowth on one occasion, and to have blubbered when he could not bring it back to life.

There is but one other person who could have been implicated, and I hesitate to name him in this place. Yet one remembers what terrific acts of misapplied courage and ferocious brutality the fanatics of history have been capable of performing when their creed and their authority have been set at naught.

III

Ellen Mary never recovered her sanity. She died a few weeks ago in the County Asylum. I hear that her husband attended the funeral. When she lost her belief in the supernal wisdom and power of

her god, her world must have fallen about her.
The thing she had imagined to be solid, real, ever-
lasting, had proved to be friable and destructible
like all other human building.

IV

The Wonder is buried in Chilborough church-
yard.

You may find the place by its proximity to the
great marble mausoleum erected over the remains
of Sir Edward Bigg, the well-known brewer and
philanthropist.

The grave of Victor Stott is marked by a small
stone, some six inches high, which is designed to
catch the foot rather than the eye of the seeker.

The stone bears the initials "V. S.," and a date
—no more.

V

I saw the Wonder before he was buried.

I went up into the little bedroom and looked at
him in his tiny coffin.

I was no longer afraid of him. His power over
me was dissipated. He was no greater and no less
than any other dead thing.

It was the same with every one. He had become

that " poor little boy of Mrs. Stott's." No one spoke of him with respect now. No one seemed to remember that he had been in any way different from other " poor little fellows " who had died an untimely death.

One thing did strike me as curious. The idiot, the one person who had never feared him living, had feared him horribly when he was dead. . . .

EPILOGUE

SOMETHING Challis has told me; something I have learned for myself; and there is something which has come to me from an unknown source.

But here again we are confronted with the original difficulty—the difficulty that for some conceptions there is no verbal figure.

It is comprehensible, it is, indeed, obvious that the deeper abstract speculation of the Wonder's thought cannot be set out by any metaphor that would be understood by a lesser intelligence.

We see that many philosophers, whose utterances have been recorded in human history—that record which floats like a drop of oil on the limitless ocean of eternity—have been confronted with this same difficulty, and have woven an intricate and tedious design of words in their attempt to convey some single conception—some conception which themselves could see but dimly when disguised in the masquerade of language; some figure that as it was limned grew ever more confused beneath the wrappings of metaphor, so that we who read can glimpse scarce a hint of its original shape and likeness. We see, also, that the very philosophers who caricatured their own eidolon, became intrigued with the logical abstraction of words and were led away into a wilderness of barren deduction—their one inspired vision of a stable premiss distorted and at last forgotten.

How then shall we hope to find words to adumbrate a philosophy which starts by the assumption that we can have no impression of reality until we have rid ourselves of the interposing and utterly false concepts of space and time, which delimit the whole world of human thought.

I admit that one cannot even begin to do this thing; within our present limitations our whole machinery of thought is built of these two original concepts. They are the only gauges wherewith we may measure every reality, every abstraction; wherewith we may give outline to any image or process of the mind. Only when we endeavour to grapple with that indeterminable mystery of consciousness can we conceive, however dimly, some idea of a pure abstraction uninfluenced by and independent of, those twin bases of our means of thought.

Here it is that Challis has paused. Here he says

that we must wait, that no revelation can reveal what we are incapable of understanding, that only by the slow process of evolution can we attain to any understanding of the mystery we have sought to solve by our futile and primitive hypotheses.

"But then," I have pressed him, "why do you hesitate to speak of what you heard on that afternoon?"

And once he answered me:

"I glimpsed a finality," he said, "and that appalled me. Don't you see that ignorance is the means of our intellectual pleasure? It is the solving of the problem that brings enjoyment—the solved problem has no further interest. So when all is known, the stimulus for action ceases; when all is known there is quiescence, nothingness. Perfect knowledge implies the peace of death, implies the state of being one—our pleasures are derived from action, from differences, from heterogeneity.

"Oh! pity the child," said Challis, "for whom there could be no mystery. Is not mystery the first and greatest joy of life? Beyond the gate there is unexplored mystery for us in our childhood. When that is explored, there are new and wonderful possibilities beyond the hills, then beyond the seas, beyond the known world, in the everyday chances and movements of the unknown life in which we are circumstanced.

"Surely we should all perish through sheer inanity, or die desperately by suicide if no mystery remained in the world. Mystery takes a thousand beautiful shapes ; it lurks even in the handiwork of man, in a stone god, or in some mighty, intricate machine, incomprehensibly deliberate and determined. The imagination endows the man-made thing with consciousness and powers, whether of reservation or aloofness ; the similitude of meditation and profundity is wrought into stone. Is there not source for mystery to the uninstructed in the great machine registering the progress of its own achievement with each solemn, recurrent beat of its metal pulse ?

"Behind all these things is the wonder of the imagination that never approaches more nearly to the creation of a hitherto unknown image than when it thus hesitates on the verge of mystery.

"There is yet so much, so very much cause for wondering speculation. Science gains ground so slowly. Slowly it has outlined, however vaguely, the uncertainties of our origin so far as this world is concerned, while the mystic has fought for his entrancing fairy tales one by one.

"The mystic still holds his enthralling belief in the succession of peoples who have risen and died—the succeeding world-races, red, black, yellow, and white, which have in turn dominated this planet. Science with its hammer and chisel may lay bare evidence, may collate material, date man's appearance, call him the most recent of placental mammals, trace his superstitions and his first conceptions of a god from the elemental fears of the savage. But the mystic turns aside with an assumption of superior knowledge ; he waves away objective evidence ; he has a certainty impressed upon his mind.

" The mystic is a power ; he compels a multitude of followers, because he offers an attraction greater than the facts of science ; he tells of a mystery profounder than any problem solved by patient investigation, because his mystery is incomprehensible even by himself; and in fear lest any should comprehend it, he disguises the approach with an array of lesser mysteries, man-made ; with terminologies, symbologies and high talk of esotericism too fearful for any save the initiate.

" But we must preserve our mystic in some form against the awful time when science shall have determined a limit ; when the long history of evolution shall be written in full, and every stage of world-building shall be made plain. When the cycle of atomic dust to atomic dust is demonstrated, and the detail of the life-process is taught and understood, we shall have a fierce need for the mystic to save us from the futility of a world we understand, to lie to us if need be, to inspirit our material and

regular minds with some breath of delicious madness. We shall need the mystic then, or the com-
pleteness of our knowledge will drive us at last to
complete the dusty circle in our eagerness to escape
from a world we understand. . . .

" See how man clings to his old and useless traditions; see how he opposes at every step the awful
force of progress. At each stage he protests that
the thing that is, is good, or that the thing that was
and has gone, was better. He despises new knowledge and fondly clings to the belief that once men
were greater than they now are. He looks back to
the more primitive, and endows it with that mystery
he cannot find in his own times. So have men ever
looked lingeringly behind them. It is an instinct,
a great and wonderful inheritance that postpones
the moment of disillusionment.

" We are still mercifully surrounded with the
countless mysteries of every-day experience, all the
evidences of the unimaginable stimulus we call life.
Would you take them away? Would you resolve
life into a disease of the ether—a disease of which
you and I, all life and all matter, are symptoms?
Would you teach that to the child, and explain to
him that the wonder of life and growth is no wonder,
but a demonstrable result of impeded force, to be
evaluated by the application of an adequate formula?

" You and I," said Challis, " are children in the infancy of the world. Let us to our play in the nursery of our own times. The day will come, perhaps, when humanity shall have grown and will have to take upon itself the heavy burden of knowledge. But you need not fear that that will be in our day, nor in a thousand years.

" Meanwhile leave us our childish fancies, our little imaginings, our hope—children that we are—of those impossible mysteries beyond the hills . . . beyond the hills."

IN THE BISON FRONTIERS OF IMAGINATION SERIES

The Wonder
By J. D. Beresford
Introduced by Jack L. Chalker

The Land that Time Forgot
By Edgar Rice Burroughs
Introduced by Mike Resnick

Omega: The Last Days of the World
By Camille Flammarion
Introduced by Robert Silverberg

Mizora: A World of Women
By Mary E. Bradley Lane
Introduced by Joan Saberhagen

Fantastic Tales
By Jack London
Edited by Dale L. Walker

The Chase of the Golden Meteor
By Jules Verne
Introduced by Gregory A. Benford

When Worlds Collide
By Philip Wylie and Edwin Balmer
Introduced by John Varley